Blurring the Lines & Extras

Amy Kaybach

Content and trigger warnings: Blurring the Lines is a novella meant for adult audiences. Content includes strong language, explicit sexual scenes, non-consensual recording of intimate situations, cheating, mention of drug and alcohol use, overdoses including that leading to death, and other mature situations.

Blurring the Lines & Extras

Edited by: Editing Fox

Edited by: Nice Girl Naughty Edits

Cover: Kimberly Sable of KBG Designs

The Blind Rebels pre-show huddle:
For the booze.
For the chicks.
For love of my sticks.
We got nothing to lose.
So bring on that booze.
The Blind Fuckin' Rebels rock!

Note To Readers

Dearest readers,

I don't want you to have any false pretenses about what's included in this book. Most of the contents have been featured elsewhere at some point in time. The main novella, *Blurring the Lines*, originally appeared in the **Rock My World** limited edition eBook anthology. Most of the items in part two were reader magnets that were (and still are) available for free in various places on the web.

The Blurring the Lines novella portrays a very different band than the one you found in the original Blind Rebels rock star romance series. In the first book, Bridging the Silence, the Blind Rebels were coming off of a year long hiatus of sorts having broken up a year before.

Blurring the Lines details what happened right before that break-up. The band at the time of the break up was already hanging by a thread and it didn't take much as you'll see to push them into a break up of epic proportions.

There are two short pieces in part two that were written exclusively for this book. They are *Sammy's V* and *The Last Angel*. I wanted to make purchasing a new book worthy of the beautiful cover made by the lovely Kimberly Sable of KBG Designs. And worthy of *your* dollars.

As for the writing of this prequel. There were so many angles I could have taken with it. Ultimately I decided on this one because it was the story that the band wanted told.

I considered making this book about Killian and Sevenya. Or even making it about how Mavrick and Callum came to form the Rebels. But neither of those were the stories that came to me easily.

This was the story that the band wanted you to know. They wanted you to know they aren't perfect and there were real problems within the band before the famed fight onstage at the Garden. They were a band struggling for years before the stage fight. Struggling with their individual pasts and with their collective loss of Sammy's sister, Sevenya.

Maybe one day, I'll write Sevenya's story. She is so much a catalyst in both this novella and in the other books of the series. Each member had a different relationship with her and her death left a different kind of mark on each member of the band. Then again maybe I'll leave Sev to rest.

For now though, it's time for me to let the Blind Rebels go as I thought I had after I finished Killian's book in the series. For now anyway.

I hope you like what I've written here and know I'm working on the next series as you enjoy this book. As always I love connecting with you all on all my social media- so feel free to reach out.

—Amy

Part One

Blurring the Lines, the Blind Rebels prequel Novella

Chapter 1

Mavrick

"Fuck yeah!" Callum screams from my balcony, wearing only a pair of tighty-whities, his hands held high over his head. "Rock and fucking roll!"

The rowdy crowd gathered at the pool below us cheers him on loudly, which only encourages the idiot. Cal turns, eyes rapidly scanning my room for something else to throw down into the pool. He locks onto the office chair since he's already chucked the TV, the balcony chair, the phone from the nightstand, and most of the clothes he was wearing. Why is it always something from my room? The fucker.

Me: Get up here. Cal's fucked up and throwing shit into the pool. Again.

Fuck if I'm paying for his shit again on this tour.

There's a knock on the door not two minutes after I send the text. I don't bother to look before pulling the door open. I know it's Jax. He was probably heading over anyway when I texted him. I'm sure hotel management is on their way up by now too.

"He's so wasted. We can't get thrown out of here before tomorrow's show."

3

Jax nods curtly, looking over my shoulder at Callum, who's out of fucking control yet again. Now he has the small glass and metal table from my balcony lifted over his head like it's some sort of victory piece.

"Darren's already working with management," Jax says as he works his way past me toward Callum, his eyes narrowed slightly on his target, who's still wielding the balcony table.

"Dude, put the table down." Jax speaks to Callum with authority, but not enough to trigger him into throwing it over the rail.

When he's high, not only is he rebellious as fuck, but he's also downright dangerous and doesn't think about consequences. It's like he's becoming the teenager he never got to be when we were in school. He was too busy working to keep himself and Killian alive, sheltered, and fed. Then in line so their aunt would keep them in her house.

But that was then. He hasn't had to worry about where their next meal was coming from for years. So I don't understand what's going on with him. Sure, with the fame came the availability of drugs, but he knows better than to do this shit. We all do.

"Cal, man..." Jax stops talking and starts moving when Callum stumbles toward the flimsy railing, still with the table over his head. He quickly grabs the light table with one hand and puts his other on Cal's shoulder, steadying the guitarist.

"Let's put the table down, bud. You don't want to hurt someone down there." He gently maneuvers it away from Callum, setting it back in the corner of the balcony. In that short amount of time, Cal manages to wiggle off his underwear and throw them off the balcony too. Now he's out there in his fucking birthday suit. Great. This is so going to be all over the internet tomorrow.

The next thing I know, Callum's got one leg over that flimsy railing on the balcony and... oh fuck me—he's going to jump into the pool again. The problem is, we're on the tenth floor this time. Not the third, like last time. Dammit.

"Callum, no!" My hollering catches Jax's attention, and when he sees what Cal's doing, he leaps, tackling my guitarist, pulling him away from the railing and falling back into my room and onto the floor. I close the sliding door and lock it. Fucking idiot.

"Fuck you, Jax, let me go. You're fired. You hear me? You are F-I-E-D. Fired." He's so fucked up. This is not the Callum I know.

I bend at the waist to get right into Callum's face while Jax still has him pinned to the floor on his back. "You can't fire him. Only I can fire him. And I thank fuck he's here. You could have killed someone, or yourself." I sigh.

"Cal, this shit is getting old," I mutter, knowing he probably won't even remember our little chat anyway.

"You want to babysit him the rest of the night, or do you want me to?" Jax huffs from the floor, still on top of a struggling Callum.

"I got him." Killian strolls in through my open door and stands over his brother splayed on the floor while he struggles with Jax. Thank God, because I did not want to foist Callum on Jax, and I sure as fuck didn't want to watch over him all night.

"Get up, asshole. It's bedtime." Killian grabs Cal under the armpits with a sneer and hauls him to his feet. "Let's go." He pushes his brother towards the door to the hall.

"Fuck you, Killian. It's not time for bed. I'm a fucking rock star. I don't have a bedtime. And you're not my father, dumbass. Our mom didn't know who he was, remember? I think he left knowing he made you," Cal tries to spit over his shoulder into the face of his twin.

Killian blinks a few times, wide eyes looking momentarily stunned and like he's going to cry at the same time, and I can't tell if it's his brother's vicious words or the spit that's thrown his way. He recovers well, though, firmly placing his dark overlord mask back on.

"Enough shit, Cal. You've had your fun destroying Mav's room. You're going to bed."

"But I can't sleep," he mutters as Killian pushes him out my door with Jax hot on their tail. I peek out the door in time to see them enter Killian's room, the door shutting as Darren turns down our hall from the elevators, his face pinched and red as he storms toward me.

"What the fuck, Mav?" he yells at me before I can pull my head back into my room.

Holding my hands up between us, I back away. Why Darren always assumes it's me, I don't know. "It wasn't me, man; Callum threw the shit off my balcony."

Darren storms past me into my room, eyeing it for more damage, no doubt. Most of the damage was done to the items that were tossed out of my room and into the pool. He even tried for my acoustic guitar that goes everywhere with me. I would have ended him if he had tossed that out, band mate or not.

"Why did you let him?" He can't seriously be blaming me for Cal's shit.

"Let him? You aren't serious, right? First, I am not his keeper. Second, he's fucking wasted. You know how crazy he gets when he's been snorting coke. He tried to jump off the balcony again, Darren. Thankfully, Jax grabbed him just in time. He was lucky last time. I'm sure he would have killed himself trying that shit from up here."

Darren runs his hand through his greasy hair and looks at me. "The label isn't going to like this."

"Fuck the label not liking it, Darren. I don't like it. Last tour, I got the bill for my room damage, most of which I didn't do. I don't want that bill again." Could I afford it? Yes. Do I want to be spending money on shit like that when it's not me doing the damage? No.

"Do you think he needs rehab?" Darren turns back to me, his weasel eyes darting around my room as he licks his lips. He's looking for paraphernalia.

I would have never thought that, of the four of us, Cal would be in this position. He'd be the last one I'd expect label management to be questioning whether rehab should be ordered. Because that comes with its own troubles. Publicity. Having to cancel shows because, like fuck, would we play without him. Cal would be the first to tell us to cut that shit out. But this tour, Cal's been over-the-top out of control. I don't know what the fuck is up with him lately.

"I'd start with cleaning up the crew. He's got to be getting the blow from somewhere."

Chapter 2

Callum

Thunk. My breath leaves me as I hit the floor.

What the hell?

My head throbs in time with my heart and now my ass hurts too. I open one eye to find an identical one staring back at me. Killian. He's so close that I can feel his hot breath on my face.

"Head hurt a little? Or is it your back?" He sneers at me, and then straddles me, robbing me of my breath. "Come on, get up!" He open-hand slaps me, just hard enough to make a point.

"Get off me, Kill." I push at him and sit up so he slides off me and onto the floor, then promptly stands with a huff. He's fully dressed already.

"Do you even realize what you did last night?" Cocking his head, he looks disappointed in me. "What you said?"

What did I do last night? I remember being bored at the pool and running into Dom from Diminished Capacity, our touring mates this tour.

Killian sighs as he drops down on the couch I must have rolled off of.

"You tried to jump off Mav's balcony. When I got there, Jax

was on top of you on the floor as you struggled and yelled profanity at Mav." Kill looks out the window of his room quickly, dropping his chin so his hair hides his eyes. But I see the tear that rolls down his face, and more than that, I feel in our twin connection that he's upset by something I said or did to him.

These days, I don't feel much of that shared connection, but I feel this. It's hurt, sadness, but it's not the swan dive I nearly took off the balcony. There is also a resignation that maybe he took what I said as truth, when really, whatever the fuck I said was just the ramblings of a wasted, exhausted rock star.

Chapter 3

Becka

"Oh my God, Becka, how did you get us these passes?" Kasey presses on the bright all-access pass around her chest. There is no way I'm telling her that I talked the KROK DJ into letting me blow him right there in the booth while he was on-air. Luckily, it was a shitty shift in the middle of the night and not many people I know would be listening then.

But I wasn't going to take no for an answer. I needed these passes to get us backstage at the Diminished Capacity/Blind Rebels co-headline show. I knew the DJ would have a way to get me where I needed to go. I simply used what God gave me to get me what I wanted. He was a typical guy, thinking with the head in his pants.

It's something I'm rather good at. Some people call it manipulative, but it's just knowing how to get what I want from people.

There's no way I'm leaving that show on Saturday alone. Neither will Kasey. She'll thank me later.

"Happy Birthday, Kase. You're so welcome. You know I'd do anything for you. We deserve this." We air-kiss each other's cheeks, as we do when we are being bougie. Kase is my best friend, always there for me, but she's a little naïve sometimes.

"This weekend is going to be so extra!" she squeals and bounces, unable to keep her excitement under wraps. "Thank you again. This fits perfectly." She winks at me, humored by her own joke.

"You're welcome." Hopefully, she'll be a little more chill on Saturday. This birthday gift is as much for me as it is for her. Sure, she'll have fun. I can guarantee it with the all-access pass.

She'll find someone she can hook up with. But I'm going for Dom from Diminished Capacity. I've loved DC since I first heard them. Dominick's voice penetrates me and makes me feel like no one else can. I can tell he knows it too because he sings directly to me. He knows we're made for each other.

We head to her birthday dinner with our other friends, at Jericho's in the heart of Chicago. They give her lame presents like bracelets and a top for her birthday. It's hard for me not to roll my eyes when she opens each one. We spend the evening enjoying three platters of appetizers and drinks all around.

It's fun, I guess, but I know that Saturday will be the real excitement. It's just Kase and me and the bands at our beck and call. I don't even know who's opening for them. Nor do I really care.

Okay, I care enough to look it up on my phone. It's some band I've never heard of...No Release. A quick web search tells me that they are some sort of chick band. Hopefully, I'll be too busy to see them anyway. By then, I should have Dominick between my legs, right where I want him.

R

WE ARE some of the first people let into the Concord, and Kase and I march right to the backstage door. I've been here before, so I know where it is. We flash our passes and are let through

11

without any wait. The guard doesn't even give us a once-over. We don't need an escort back or anything. I'll have to thank that DJ the next time I see him. He really came through. It's amazing what a talented pair of lips like mine can get you in this town. I flip my hair over my shoulder as we make our way farther backstage. This is exactly where I belong.

At first, Kase and I stick together, wandering the halls backstage like we know what we are doing, who we are looking for. We find the shared dressing room for No Release first. The two guys in the room look tense. One girl mean-mugs the other, who seems oblivious to her counterpart's stares. Yikes. One of the guys, the one with a guitar on his lap, looks up at me and smiles, so I wave. He nods back, and the others in the room turn toward the door, but there's no way I am going in there. Not with the uncomfortable tension spilling out into the hall. It's not like I care about this band anyway. Chick bands aren't my bag.

We head farther into the bowels of the backstage area. I've never been back this far at the Concord. Who knew there were so many rooms? We find some marked as the dressing rooms for the Rebels. They all seem to have their own rooms. Duly noted.

The music from the stage vibrates my body by the time we find the rooms marked off for Diminished Capacity. Zedd, the drummer, has his door closed. He's so elusive. He's not my type, so it doesn't really matter anyway.

We move past the door with the drummer's name, toward another door. This one is marked with just a guitar. Ashton's the guitarist for DC. He's almost too pretty. His shoulder-length blonde hair hangs just right, and he always looks a little too put together. I like my men more rogue, a little rough and tumble.

Across the hall from his door is another one labeled Logan for the bassist, and a known player. No way I'd be caught dead with him. He's obviously not looking for anything more than a quick fuck, but Kasey thinks he's cute. Her eyes grow to the size of saucers as she reaches out a hand and brushes her fingertips to the very door that holds her favorite bassist. She's so starstruck, I'd be amused if I wasn't still looking forward to my rendezvous with Dom.

"You should knock and introduce yourself," I urge her. "I'm going to see Dom." I nod my head toward the door with a security guard stationed outside. Dom's door, no doubt. He probably needs security 24/7 because of all the girls who want him.

She hesitates at Logan's door, but I keep going until I'm at Dom's. I can't be bothered with Kasey when I feel Dominick pulling me down the hall. He knows I'm here. I reach up to knock on the door, when Brutus, the security dude, grabs my hand and stops my hand mid-knock.

"Dominick is not seeing guests tonight, miss." He barely looks at me, the asshole. Surely, he sees that I'm the one exception to that rule.

"But it's me, Becka. He knows I'm here. He's expecting me."

"Look, chickie, every night I get a list of people who are okay to let in. Tonight, Dom was specific when he said nobody," this overpaid bouncer roars at me. "There is no one on the list tonight. Bug off before we have your credentials revoked and you get eighty-sixed from the arena altogether." He takes a sideways step, effectively blocking my access to the door.

"But…" Clearly, he doesn't understand that Dominick and I have a standing engagement when he's in town.

"There are no buts, no exceptions. Get lost." He fixes his gaze straight ahead, dismissing me. He has no idea how pissed Dom would be if he knew Brutus was acting like this.

The door behind Brutus flies open, and Dominick stands there staring at me intently with his light blue eyes such a contrast to his dark hair.

"What the actual fuck is going on out here? I'm trying to get ready for the show." He looks between me and Brutus.

"Sorry, sir. This girl believes she has an appointment with you, and I was trying to explain that no one is to be let through tonight." Brutus stands up a little straighter now that Dom is here. All I see is Dom. I can look nowhere else.

His gaze finally shifts my way again, and he looks me over in my short, black, ruffled skirt and my tight black Diminished Capacity t-shirt, tied so my taut midriff peeks out, showing my pierced navel. He loves a pierced navel. I watch as his eyes travel the length of my legs, which look spectacular, thanks to the black fuck-me stilettos I'm wearing.

"I have no appointments. Quit pestering my security detail." His eyes narrow at me.

"But it's me, Dom. It's Becka." I flick my hair, trying to remember how I looked the last time we were together.

"I don't know who the fuck you are, but if it will keep you quiet, come in." He holds the door open wider, and I slip into the dressing room. I'm about to remind him who I am, when he turns back to Brutus.

"No more interruptions. Got it, B?" Brutus gives Dom a curt nod before closing the door.

The dressing room is kind of boring. It's just a plain white room with a nice vanity and table. A private bathroom off to the side and a simple chair and matching brown loveseat finish off the space. There's a guitar propped up in the corner and some clothes are laid out, like maybe he's supposed to change before heading to the stage, but his tight jeans and black t-shirt look just right on him. There's no window to the outside or anything.

"Dom..." When I say his name, his eyes dilate and darken. Oh, he wants me. Just like I knew he would. It's all part of my plan. I knew he'd remember me.

"Hey, you want a line before we get things started?" He gestures to the vanity, where I see a few lines of coke and a razor right on the surface.

"Uh, sure." I haven't done coke before, but why not. "When in Rome," I mutter as I walk over to the table.

He hands me a straw. "Rome? Is that where we've met before?" His question is honest. See, I knew he'd remember me, just not from where. I relax a little since he does know who I am.

"No, not Rome." I can't help my giggle. "That's just a saying."

"Have you done this before?" He narrows his eyes on mine. When I shake my head, he asks if I'm sure I want to do it. I nod.

"Like this," he says as he grabs my mini straw from me and demonstrates by leaning over the vanity and snorting a line quickly up his nose. Handing me back the straw, he nods to me. "Go ahead."

I mimic what Dom did and snort the line, my nose burning instantly as the fire moves to the back of my throat.

"Good, right?" He sniffs as I nod, the burning in my nose and throat getting worse and causing my eyes to water. I'm not sure what I'm supposed to feel now, but I really feel just kind of numb, like normal. "Just give it a minute. You'll start to feel it."

He pulls me to him and kisses me hard, just as a jolt of electricity starts humming under my skin. I knew it would be like this between us. I kiss him back, him letting my tongue explore his mouth, while my hands move across his chest and around his back to pull him toward me.

This energy moves between us, through us, tingling the whole way. Is that what Dom was talking about, the tingling?

I want nothing more than to complete our connection and show him how much we belong together. I press myself against his erection, reveling in the fact that he's hard for me.

I'm doing this to Dom.

"Oh yeah, I have exactly what you need, baby." He reaches behind me, unhooking my bra, then working my shirt and bra off over my head together. As soon as my shirt's tossed to the side, he licks my breast roughly, and lightning zings through my body, striking right between my legs. I press them together, trying to put out the fire. I need him inside me.

He groans. "Fuck, baby, you're hot." He moves to the other and sucks, causing that familiar wetness between my thighs.

Reaching between my legs, he slips a finger under the band of my barely-there thong and runs it down my seam. "God, you're so ready, aren't you?" He slips it inside me easily and saws in and out a few times.

He has no idea how much I've dreamed of this day. Since the first time I saw him on stage at RockFest Illinois and every day in between. With each push of his finger, I clench hard, showing him just how good the real thing will be. Because it's so happening, and soon.

"Oh! Dom." I take matters into my hands and reach for his fly to undo it with my trembling fingers. "I need you. Now."

When he pulls out his finger, I whimper, not wanting to lose the connection between us. "Don't worry, I've got exactly what you need, baby." I wish he'd just give it to me, then. He pushes my underwear down to my knees, and then grabs his pants from my trembling hands and frees himself.

I briefly wonder if he'll even fit inside me, but he pushes my skirt up over my hips, lines himself up and pushes in without warning. There's a pinch because he's bigger than what I'm used to, and he doesn't really give me any time to get used to him before he's out and pounding back into me again. And again. Each push pins my back firmly against the wall next to the bathroom.

He grunts with each thrust, and my back scrapes up the cool concrete of the wall, and then back down slightly when he withdraws most of the way. My back's going to be rubbed raw at this rate.

It's Dom, I repeat to myself silently. I love Dom and he loves me. Fuck, he is loving me.

Seeming to understand I need a little something more, he leans in and lightly grazes my nipple with his teeth, and the slight bite of pain adds exactly what I need. I can't help the groan I release against his neck as I firmly scratch my nails down his back.

"Ugh, Dom. Harder." My words are all he needs to really start thundering into me. I don't feel the wall against my back anymore, or the roughness of the slide up and down. I feel him and only him everywhere.

I don't even have words anymore. My high-pitched squeaks are getting louder as his movements go wild, just like I wanted. This is even better than I imagined.

Normally, I'd have come by now, but the connection between us doesn't escalate. Instead, it just keeps going. There just isn't quite enough to get me to the peak and push me over. He feels so good, but I'm just not getting there, even when I swirl to rub myself against his pelvic bone, begging for more friction. But he just keeps thrusting and thrusting.

He grunts with another hard thrust, and he's pulsating. I move against him frantically, trying to get mine. I'm almost there.

"Ugh, Dom...no!" He pulls out and away, even though I'm obviously not done. I whine in disappointment and reach down to take things into my own hands. I want to come too—ugh, fuck. He watches me trying to get off, seemingly amused at my attempt.

"It's the coke, babe. Don't worry about it. I'll take care of you after the show and make sure you get off real good." He pulls his pants up and tucks his shirt in.

When he opens the door, he leaves me exposed to anyone who happens by, my shirt and bra across the room, my underwear around my knees and my skirt hiked up over my hips with my hand between my legs. I'm trying to get myself there, but since Dom pulled out, I'm just not getting any further along.

"Let her clean herself up," he says to Brutus over his shoulder before heading down the hall, the door closing behind him.

Just like that, he's gone, and I'm only left with the buzzing under my skin and my blood racing in my ears as the excitement starts to ebb. I give up on my orgasm and hobble into the bathroom to clean myself up.

Back in the dressing room, I put my bra and shirt back on.

There's a knock on the door, and then Brutus sticks his head into the room. "Your friend Kasey is out here."

I nod and head to the door. "Hey, Kase."

"Oh my God, Becka. Look." She holds up a handful of guitar picks, each one different. "He gave these to me." She slips her new treasures into her purse. "Is Dom still in there?" She peeks around me, trying to get a glimpse of my boyfriend. She must know what we just did, even I can smell it in the room.

I shake my head.

"I think they are going on first tonight, before the Rebels. Logan was telling me they switch nights back and forth. Let's go watch them! Diminished Capacity!" Her squeal reverberates through my head and not in a pleasant way. She takes my hand and drags me to the side of the stage, where we stand as DC starts their first song.

We sway and sing along loudly, because it's not like anyone can hear us over the band anyway. But Dom never so much as glances my way. I wonder if Kase had any luck with Logan the way I did with Dom. I have a feeling she didn't. I don't think she's the type to make the first move. She doesn't understand that you must make the first move with these rocker guys. If you don't, they'll move along to someone who will. Oh well. Her loss... definitely not mine. I got Dom and am getting some more after the show.

I can't wait until after the show when Dom and I will finish what we started. I press my legs together, still turned on, still needing relief. He promised me. And Dom would never go back on his promise.

The band comes off stage from doing their encore and rush past us in a flurry of activity. Instruments and monitors are handed off to waiting crew members and are rushed over to the VIP. Those are the hussies who pay for an autograph and photo. They aren't special, just paying customers, so they must be dealt with. It's ridiculous that the record company makes DC lower themselves to this kind of activity. I guess even they have to keep their fans happy, and these days the groupies are all over-entitled wenches. We stick around and watch a few minutes of the Rebels as they play.

"Isn't Callum adorable?" Kase gushes. What is it with her and guitarists? Everyone knows that they are all show, no go. I'm all about Mavrick when it comes to the Rebels. He's got charisma for days. Plus, he's way hotter, with that choppy hair sticking out here and there.

I shrug. "I guess. I'm more of a Mav girl when it comes to the Rebels." Halfway through the Rebels show, I know that Dom must be done with the VIP ticket holders.

On the way down the hall, Kase pops into their green room and sits on the couch near Logan. But Dominick is missing from the green room. He's probably wondering where I am. Brutus stands at his post outside the door.

"Um, can I just go in this time?" I look at him and bat my eyes.

"Are you sure you want to?" he asks. His face is trying to tell me something, but I can't figure out what it is.

"Yes."

"Be my guest." He opens the door, and I walk in.

The smell of pot and sex assault me the moment I walk in. Dom looks up from behind the loveseat at me and smiles widely, his face stretching out oddly. "There you are. We got tired of waiting, but we just started."

We? It's then I notice the stark-naked girl he has bent over the brown loveseat, and he continues to thrust in and out of her as he speaks to me like we're all just talking about sports scores or weather or what to have for lunch.

"What's wrong, baby? Don't you want to join us?" He cocks his head at me with a smug look on his face as he thrusts into her slowly, causing her to moan and push back toward him.

"Darlene here doesn't mind, do ya, babe?" He slaps her ass as he pulls out, and she winces slightly as she shakes her head and then glances up at me.

"It's Dar-la!" Her voice goes up a register when he thrusts back into her, and she moans and rubs back against him again. "Dom, just fuck me. Please." Her keening sounds so desperate. That's not what I sound like.

"I am fucking you, darlin'." He drags out slow, before thrusting hard into her again. "This one is going to get you off, and then you can return the favor. What was your name again?" He looks at me, hopeful, but they never stop having sex. He stands behind her, one hand on her back, thrusting lazily in and out while she groans and undulates with each thrust. Her hand moves toward her own apex, and he swipes it away.

"No! Leave that for her." His eyes meet mine, and he smiles at me wickedly. "Come on, sweetheart, help her come now, and she'll help you when it's your turn. We'll do it against the wall like before."

I can't think. All I feel is the acid working its way slowly up my throat with each of Dom's thrusts into Darla. He was in me only a few hours ago. I'm his true love, and he's mine, but now he's ruining it by fucking someone else right in front of my eyes.

"Come on, babe." He bites his lip and moans. "We'll work you over together real good, making sure you get yours this time, just like I promised. But first, Darlene here needs your help to come." He flicks his hips into her, a little more forcefully this time, and she moans and bites the loveseat. She looks me over with lust-filled eyes. "Darlene loves to play, right, babe?"

"Dar! La!" she spits breathlessly, eyes rolling back before focusing on me and nodding while she moistens her lips with her tongue, eyeing my hand. She really wants me touching her like that?

He pulls out and pumps himself slowly while lasciviously grinning at me. He's abandoned her again so she squirms against the couch. My heart pounds in my ears, and I blink, wishing that it was just me and Dom in here.

"Dom! I need to fucking come!" She winces when he starts pounding back into her hard right in front of me, each thrust causing another crack in my black heart.

I want to leave, but I'm stuck here watching him destroy my heart as he keeps pushing into her and watching my reactions.

"Come on, babe," she whines at me between pants, her eyes locking with mine as she leans up, tugging on her nipples. Wanting me to see it. "Do me a solid, ugh, and help me finish. Ugh." She looks down at where my hands are fisted at my sides and nods again, trying to encourage me to touch her. Down there. "Just do me like you'd do yourself. Ugh, please."

Dom laughs. "She knows all about touching herself. Don't you, babe?" He left me wanting as part of his cruel game. That fucker.

Darla winces again and shifts against the couch as he starts pumping in and out of her, and then stops again to stroke himself as he watches me. I thought he loved me. This should be for me. Not her.

"Dom, she's not helping," she whines, shifting more against the couch. "Please, I need more. Stop fucking edging me." She doesn't complete the sentence, and he's in her again, setting a blistering pace.

"Ughh. More. Ugh. Dammit. Dom. More." She drags out the 'M' as he shoves his free hand between her and the couch while she squeezes her nipples hard again. Her lips pucker into an obscene 'O'. That's what I needed him to do to me. Why is she getting this and not me? He's supposed to love me.

"Yesss," she hisses like the snake she is.

"Oh God," she cries loudly as I mutter it at the same time. I can't watch this anymore. I turn.

"Finally," she sighs and lays against the couch like an old, abandoned doll, spent.

I bolt out of the room. I run blindly down the hall with Brutus's laugh chasing me. "I tried to warn you."

I make twists and turns in the labyrinth of the backstage area until I find a bathroom. Pushing into the single seat bathroom, I puke the burning acid that had been threatening to spill since walking in on Dom and his concubine. After I'm done purging, I slide to the floor, pull my knees to my chest, drop my head, and cry.

Chapter 4

Mavrick

Cal's been a sullen fucker all day, avoiding me for the most part, refusing to acknowledge my existence when he can't avoid me. I'm not sure if he's embarrassed about last night or what, but the only time he even bothered to look at me was when we were on stage tonight. Then he was like his normal self. The rock God personified. That is the Callum I know. The guy who's all about the music. He's a hell of a songwriter and guitar player. Or at least he is when he's not trying to throw himself off my balcony in a drug and alcohol induced frenzy.

He didn't miss a note and didn't appear wasted onstage, so I am leaning toward him being embarrassed.

I mean, he's worked his ass off to get here right alongside the rest of the band, if not harder. He's always been the one to keep us together, to keep us sane in the crazy rock world we live in.

We sell millions of albums. People come to see us play and stand in line to file into the concert venues. All the girls want him. But all he seems to want lately is coke. And when it's not coke, it's alcohol with a side of pot. Sometimes it's all three.

It's the coke that makes him act like a fucking lunatic. I'm not going to lie; him trying to propel himself off my balcony scared the shit out of me last night. It was funny when we were only three floors up. It wasn't funny from ten floors. Thank God, Jax grabbed him before he actually jumped. Half a second later, and who knows what the fuck would have happened. He'd either have hurt or killed himself. There is no way that pool was deep enough, and that's if he'd make it to the pool and not splat on the concrete.

He's really starting to worry me. Touring isn't all sunshine and roses. It's hard on all of us, and we all have our ways of coping. But the twins don't seem to be coping well at all. Killian's fucking everything with a pussy that comes within five feet of him. I just pray he's wrapping up or it will rot the fuck off. And Cal's the same way, only instead of burying himself in a woman, he's snorting a hill of coke.

Cocaine isn't coping, though. If things don't get better soon, we'll have to fucking send him to rehab like we did Sammy's sister. We all know how that turned out. You never forget the first time you see a dead body. I know that for a fact, because sometimes, Seven's dead body haunts my dreams. Still. Which is why his cocaine-fueled death wish doesn't make sense to me.

I can't fucking imagine what Sammy goes through if it's like this for me years later. That was his sister. And fuck, he loved her. We all did. She was a good kid, broken more than we knew, and trying to cope with things no one should ever have to cope with.

Sammy confided in me some of the shit he found in her diary. Things he didn't know happened to her. He still beats himself up about not realizing what she was going through. I don't think he's mentioned it to the other guys, so it stays locked up in the vault in my head. I'd never tell anyone else, unless he wanted me to.

I slip out of our green room. We have to be on the bus in

another ninety minutes, but I wander the maze-like halls of the backstage area, looking for a peaceful place to just be alone for a bit, before I have to load up and be on the sardine can they call our bus with the guys for a sixteen-hour drive to the next venue. I am pretty damn sure that Callum will be a cantankerous fuck on the drive. I love my Rebel brothers, but sometimes I get sick of all the togetherness.

When I haven't seen anybody I know for a few minutes, I start to look for a john. I should have pissed before I decided to go wandering. I finally find one that I push into, only to see a blonde woman sitting in a ball, hugging her knees to her chest, and sobbing loudly.

I should just back the fuck out of the room quietly and head back the way I came, before she catches sight of me. I'm allergic to crying chicks and their drama, but something about the scene tugs at my fucking heartstrings. Weird. I didn't think I had any of those.

"Um, are you okay?" I squat down so I am on her level and am rewarded when she lifts her head and looks at me. She's utterly stunning, even though there are two black rivers of mascara running down her face.

Her eyes are a clear but watery light blue and framed by her sandy blonde hair. It's probably from a bottle because the shade is too perfect. It has a slight wave to it.

She doesn't speak. She just shakes her head slowly, letting me know that she is, indeed, not okay. Hence the tears.

"Are you injured? Do you need the police?" I look her over quickly, just to make sure. She seems to be okay, best I can tell, there's no blood or visible wounds. But who knows what's led her to this point, where she is bawling, curled up in a ball on the filthy floor of a backstage bathroom.

I don't recognize her, and we've been on the road long enough with this current touring package that I know most of them and their girls by sight should they wander around backstage. She's definitely not a crew member, not dressed like that. She's no one's girl I know of either.

She shakes her head again, then rests her chin on her knees and stares at me quietly.

"Um, do you want some water?" Not knowing what else to do, I shove the sealed water bottle I've been carrying toward her.

This time, she nods and reaches a shaky hand toward me. I make a show of breaking the seal of the bottle before handing it to her, so she knows it's safe to drink from. She takes a few dainty sips, and then recaps it.

"Thank you." Her voice is quiet and solemn. "I appreciate it."

She starts to unfold and stretches out her bare legs. She's wearing a super short black skirt, and I glance away before I see something I probably shouldn't. I mean, she's obviously upset. I shouldn't be trying to peek up her skirt.

"My boyfriend, or ex-boyfriend now, is a dick!" she proclaims as she pushes herself up to stand. "Can you believe I caught him back here... doing sex things with someone else. And when I caught them... he had the nerve to ask me if I wanted to join in!" Her voice is both pissed and incredulous as she raises her eyebrows and watches my face for a reaction.

"Seriously?" I don't know who her boyfriend is, or was, but dude must have low standards because that's beyond anything even I'd do. And I've admittedly done some low things.

She nods and regards me as she leans against the bathroom wall.

"Damn. I'm sorry. That's not the way a man is supposed to act." I hate apologizing because some other man's been an asshole.

She shrugs her left shoulder and looks down and back up at me.

"We've been dating for years. I just can't believe he'd treat

26

me like that. I don't deserve that. He's probably been cheating on me the whole time." Her sudden anger at the way she's been treated is warranted. I don't care who you are, you don't deserve that. There's nothing worse than a cheater. I know. My dad cheated on my mom all the time. And what's worse? She took him back each and every time.

I nod at her. "You don't. No one does. He sounds like a real winner." I roll my eyes to emphasize just how not cool his actions are.

"Well, it's definitely over between us." She brushes her hands together. "I can't stand to even think about him. Not after what I saw. And that he wanted me to fucking join him. So gross." She looks up at me, our eyes locking.

There is a weird chemistry in the air between us that I'm having trouble reading. Usually, girls throw themselves at me. I mean, I'm the lead singer in the Blind fucking Rebels. Everyone's heard of us.

I'm intensely attracted to her, but I can't tell if it's due to my hero complex kicking in and wanting me to save the sad girl, or actual physical attraction. It's odd, and I think she recognizes my hesitation. It's not like I can do much anyway, considering that I leave town in just over an hour.

"As it should be. Never give anyone your self-respect." I sound like a fucking shrink. Or I think I do. I've never been to one, so I don't really know. They wanted me to see one in high school, because I didn't fit in and didn't do well in school. It's because I just wanted music, not to learn history.

"Those are wise words. I'll keep them in mind." She continues to stare at me in a way that makes me feel hot and bothered. What the hell is wrong with me? This girl was crying two minutes ago.

"My name is Becka, by the way." She reaches out her hand to shake mine. Her hand is dainty, and she turns it over as if to have me kiss it. She wants me to kiss her. I probably look like the perfect rebound fuck. Hell, I probably *am* the perfect rebound, so why am I hesitating? My gut's usually never wrong, but I override it and bring her small, soft hand to my lips and leave a barely-there kiss.

"Mavrick Slater, but my friends call me Mav." She blushes slightly. She knows exactly who I am. As a matter of fact, I'm pretty sure I saw her watching our show from the side of the stage. That means she has backstage credentials, courtesy of someone. Which means the fuckin' ex must be a crew guy. Or I guess she could be in a relationship with someone in our opener, No Release, but I seriously doubt that.

"Hey, you want to get away from this place for a while? You could come on our bus. Hit the road and get away from this town."

What the fuck did I just suggest to this total stranger? And what in the hell was I thinking? Sometimes I say the stupidest shit when I'm in awkward situations, and this time is no exception.

She seems to be weighing it like it was a legit offer, and I guess it kind of was. There is something about her that isn't like the usual fans who are always trying to grab at one of us. Maybe it was that she wore her vulnerability on her sleeve. Maybe it was that I just want to play the hero and make everything right in her world.

"You're serious?" Her eyes narrow slightly, as if she can't tell if I'm playing her or not.

I nod slowly. "Yes. It's a long ride to the next show. Sixteen hours. Our bus is kind of loud and crazy sometimes, but yes. You are more than welcome. And I mean it in the most gentlemanly of ways. You can take one of the empty bunks—we have two of them."

She looks through her purse and pulls out her phone. "Do you have a charger I can borrow?"

It looks like an iPhone like mine, so I nod.

"Then okay." She nods, shooting out a text to someone. "Can you do me one favor, though?"

"Sure, whatcha need?" Stupid Mav. She could be asking for money or something. Never say sure. Ask and then say sure once you find out if the favor is reasonable.

"Can you go into the Diminished Capacity green room and ask for Kasey and give her these?" She hands me a set of keys. "She can take my car home. She's my best friend and roomie, and she's in love with Logan, so she's hanging out with them. I totally trust her with my car. I've already texted her that I'm going on your bus."

I half-wonder if this Kasey person isn't going to jump me and demand I bring her along too. I've been in this business long enough to see a little of everything. So it wouldn't surprise me.

"It's just my ex might be in there with her, and I don't want to let him know what I'm doing. She knows the score. Just tell her to check her phone and that I've asked you to deliver my keys." She nods at me as we start back toward the area backstage that is populated.

Not knowing what the fuck I'm doing, I walk into the DC greenroom, wondering which of these fuckers might be her ex. "Is there a Kasey in here?"

A pretty brunette's head whips my way, her frosted pink lips parting as she lifts her hand. "Um, I'm Kasey."

I hand her the keys. "Your friend Becka said she texted you and that you'd know what to do."

She looks briefly a. the keys I've bestowed upon her, and then nods discreetly. "Yes. Tell her I understand."

"Uh, thanks?" I'm not sure why I'm thanking her, but it seems like the appropriate thing to do.

"No problem. Great show tonight, by the way." She smiles up at me, and I swear I see stars in her eyes. Kind of like the fans get. With a little bit of awe mixed with lust.

"Hey, thanks. Well, see ya." I mean probably, not really, but it's a way to excuse myself quickly from the room. She's already turned back to the guy in DC, Logan. I hope she knows what she's doing with him. He's more of a man-whore than Killian is.

I return to the hall, half expecting not to see Becka, but she's there, standing against the wall, nervously looking toward the opposite end of the hall.

"Come on, babe. Let's head to the bus and get you situated." She grabs my hand as if she's worried we might get separated and I'll suddenly forget who she is. Like her ex did.

Chapter 5

Mavrick

Sammy and Callum are already on the bus when we come walking in. "Sam, Cal, this is my friend Becka. Becka, that's Sam, our drummer, and Cal, our guitarist. I'm not sure where Killian's at." I look up at Callum, specifically. They are twins, after all.

"I'm not my brother's keeper. I don't know where the fuck he is either." Callum just shrugs. "But it's about time you lay off mother-henning me." He flops onto the couch with a joint in his hand.

"Not with guests on the bus, please." I nod toward his blunt.

"Not with guests on the bus, please." He mimics me in a ridiculous voice as he rolls his eyes, but he tucks the lighter in his other hand.

"Thanks, man." I acknowledge his action.

"Fuck off," he says as he flips me the bird in his now empty hand.

I just shake my head, then escort Becka to the back lounge on our bus. She doesn't need to be exposed to whatever the fuck is wrong with Cal.

We usually use the back room on our bus to write when

31

we're inspired or mess around with video games. Sometimes someone will shack up in here because they have a girl or a need to be left the fuck alone, away from everyone else. That's me right now. Both of them. I'm antsy because I'm not sure what to expect from Becka. I figure this will be a more private place to gauge our expectations.

"We can hang in here for a while. Watch TV or play video games." I grab some of the clothes and crap that's laying around. "Sorry, Sammy is like living with a teenager. He never puts his shit where it goes."

She kind of giggles and sits on the edge of the couch as I throw his stuff in one of the empty bunks, and then close the door between the lounge and the rest of the bus.

"Can I get you something to drink? We have Coke, Diet Coke, Gatorade, coffee, water, beer, various liquors."

"Oh, um, another water would be nice." Her tongue darts out and moistens those red lips of hers.

I close her in the lounge and go to the full-size fridge to get a couple of cold bottles of water.

Killian's now spread out on the couch in the main area with Cal and Sam. He nods at me. "Glad you're getting some tonight. It's been a while." Why the fuck are these guys keeping track? I flip him the bird and hear his deep, dry chuckle as I return to Becka.

"Thanks." She takes the new bottle of water. "So, um... I've never been in a tour bus before." She looks around the room.

"Some bands put a queen-size bed back here. Ours has a pull-out for entertaining. But usually, it's just a couple of us back here either playing music or video games. Or chilling." I don't tell her that Cal used to come back here and read sometimes, when he just wanted to be alone, but he doesn't do that much anymore.

"It's cozy." She scoots slightly closer to me. "So where are we going, exactly?"

"Next show is in Atlanta. It'll take us about sixteen hours to get there. Mostly because our driver will have to stop and sleep. They can't drive straight through. They have logs they have to fill out. It's a whole thing."

"That's so cool. I've never been there. This is going to be so much fun. Thank you for this. I really did need it. You have no idea. I just want to leave my life for a bit, and this is the perfect way to do it." She puts her hand on my thigh, and I am trying to figure out her intentions. I mean, she was bawling not even two hours ago because she caught her boyfriend cheating on her.

Now she's sitting here, touching me. I think she might be putting the moves on me, but then again, she could just be one of those overly touchy-feely chicks. Hard to tell.

Granted, I feel an intense and immediate attraction to her. It zings through my thigh where she touches me and squeezes lightly. Becka is stunning in a very classic sort of way. Beautiful long blonde hair with just the right amount of wave. Her gorgeous light blue eyes are a shade I haven't seen on a person before. They are the color of a shallow Caribbean Sea. And those full luscious lips are painted deep red.

I shift in my seat. She knows she's attractive, and I think she's using it to her advantage. I've never brought a girl along with us before. This is not a Mav thing to do. I don't even know her. Sure, I've sown my oats on the road here and there—I'm a damn rock star and my oats have needs, but I certainly don't bring them on long-haul bus rides. I'm not Killian.

Last tour, he had a stage-four clinger and made the mistake of bringing her on for a twelve-hour trip. By the time we got to our destination, he had to have Jax physically remove her. All because he wanted someone to occupy his time on the trip.

Maybe Callum is the one who needs to get laid. He'd probably lay off the drugs if he had some sex. I might suggest that to him. Of course, knowing Callum lately, he'd likely attempt to deck me if I suggest he get laid.

She squeezes my thigh harder, bringing me back to the here and now. I don't understand how I can be both insanely attracted, yet also weary of her.

"So, Mav," she purrs as she swings her legs toward me, practically sitting on my lap. If that's not a sign that the light is green, I don't know what is. "What can I do for you?" She cocks her head at me and smiles. "I want to thank you for bringing me on the road with you. And being so tender with me." She leans up and gently places a kiss on my cheek and fuck if it doesn't travel right to my dick too. Her hand caresses my chest.

I groan and shake my head. My dick is telling me to get to work. My brain is telling me I barely know this girl.

She kisses my lips gently, and then peppers my jaw with more kisses, her hand never stopping the caressing of my chest. "I'm on the pill so we can bareback it. I'm totally clean," she whispers before nibbling on my ear.

As enticing as that sounds, there is one thing I never do, and that's bareback it. I may be a rock star, and I certainly love the sex that comes freely with that, but I'm not risking my life on barebacking it with this or any other girl. And that's just the health aspect of it. I also don't want any little Mavs or Mavettes coming back to haunt me. I've used rubbers since I started having sex in high school. I'm not naïve. I'm not fatherhood material and I know that for a fact.

"I'm more than willing, but I never make love without a glove, darling. It's not that I don't trust you, but I really, really don't want a kid."

She shrugs. "Suit yourself." She lifts her shirt over her head and unleashes her breasts from her frilly white bra. "Like what you see?" She lifts them up and smiles at me. "All-natural." She gives them a caress, and that disintegrates whatever threads of self-restraint I had left.

I lean in and take one in my mouth, causing her to moan and arch her back, basically shoving her tits at me. And she's right, they are all-fucking-natural and fantastic. She whimpers when I release it, but fully straddles my lap and runs her hands up my shirt, gently scratching her nails against my chest. I rid myself of my shirt, and she grips my shoulders hard as soon as I do, grinding herself hard against my crotch when I take the other tit between my lips.

The more I suck, the harder she grinds herself against me. Judging by her moans, she's pretty damn close to getting herself off, and damn if that doesn't cause my cock to strain against my jeans as it hardens, demanding that he be let out to play. The fucker in my pants is pissed off it isn't the one making her come. Fuck, he's hard and angry she's doing this herself.

I lift her little skirt and slip a finger into her little frilly thong. The instant my finger makes contact with her clit, she digs her nails into my shoulders, body tensing, head thrown back. "Oh fuck. Yes!" All of her muscles tighten as her eyes roll back. Damn, she's a sight when she comes.

I help her lie back on the couch, and she moans with a slight smile on her face, her eyes hooded.

"That was fuckin' hot to watch, but now I want in. I hope you're okay with that."

Her eyes meet mine. "Yes, please. I want all of you. I need more." She rubs her thighs together at the thought. I stand and push out of my pants. As soon as my cock is free, she's reaching for it and gives it a squeeze, and then another, causing me to flex my hips forward.

She takes my flexing as an invitation and leans in to take me into her mouth. Oh, fuck yeah. She sucks like a pro. This girl knows her way around a fucking blow job, that's for sure. I'm already about to blow my wad. I really wanted to come inside her, but this feels too damn good to stop. I can't help but piston my hips at her face, resting my hand on the back of her head.

"Oh fuck, you're amazing." She tries to reply around my dick, and the extra vibration pushes me over the edge unexpectedly. I don't even have time to warn her, but she just swallows, then sits back on her heels and wipes her mouth across the back of her hand.

"Now we're even." She smiles up at me. "But I hope we're not done."

"Just give me a second." She nods, but leans in and kisses her way up my chest, up my neck, and finally pushes up on her toes to land one on my mouth. Her arms come around me and she caresses my ass cheeks as she presses her chest into mine, drawing her nipples along my torso. That wakes my cock right the fuck back up.

It doesn't take me long before I'm yearning to be inside her, and she lets me know I'm not alone in that.

"Please, tell me you have a rubber," she says as she rubs herself against my bare leg. "'Cause I need you in me, like, now." She reaches between her legs and slowly rubs herself, moaning as she does.

I grab one out of the drawer and make short work of sheathing myself before I sit back on the couch. Damn if she's going to get off without me deep inside her again. I hold myself with one hand while helping her line herself up.

She lowers herself onto me so slowly, and it's all I can do to keep myself from shoving up hard to meet her.

The farther down she gets, the more she moans, her head falling back slightly. "So good."

Once she settles on my lap, I grip her hips, and she starts to swirl them. "Oh God. Oh, fuck yeah." She moves in slow bucking motions at first, moving faster and moaning louder as she goes.

It's so fucking sexy, the way she bucks against me and squeezes her breasts.

As good as she feels like this, I want her on her hands and knees with me balls deep. I stop her undulations and move us, so her ass is in the air and her chest and face are on the couch.

I slide into her from behind, and she immediately pushes up against me. Yes. This is exactly what I needed. I run a hand up her back and lean over her, kissing her behind the ear. "You are amazing. I'm so fucking hard right now, it hurts," I whisper, and she pushes back against me again.

I can't help myself. I need her, and I take her. She slides up slightly on the couch with each of my thrusts, her moans louder with each one. She flails an arm out and grips the throw pillow, then bites it as she pushes her chest into the couch as I push in. I reach around and squeeze those perfect breasts. Her breath sucks in, and she whines out, "Yes. Mav. Harder." Then pushes back against me.

Fuck, she's not holding back, and I can't either. I give those breasts a final pinch on the nipple before I let go to hold those perfect hips of hers. It's like they are made for me to hold on to while I fuck her.

I continue thrusting in and out faster, until she starts to tighten around me. The base of my spine tingles, so I slip a hand between her and the couch and swipe at her clit in a steady circle until all of her muscles tense around me hard.

"Fuck, fuck, fuck, ooh fuuuuuuck... Mav. Ugh." Her voice starts as a hoarse whisper and ramps up into a loud, whiny, extended cry. A few more thrusts, and I curse as I shoot my load. My balls ache with each pulse as I weaken and collapse on top of her back, trying to catch my breath.

"Fuck, that was hot," I pant out quietly.

She murmurs her agreement into the couch cushion. Realizing I'm probably crushing her, I sit up on my knees. Pulling on my clothes, I hit the small bathroom in the lounge area. I start the shower and return to Becka, who's curled up onto the couch now, half asleep. She's pulled my t-shirt up over her like a blanket, which gives me an idea. I step into the hallway and grab myself some clothes.

I grab her a shirt and a pair of Blind Rebels sweatpants.

She'll swim in them, but it's all I have for her. She'll be more comfortable, and the guys in the front of the bus won't get an eyeful should she go to the bathroom.

I return to the lounge and set the clothes down.

"Hey, beautiful. Wake up. Let's take a shower." She nods and sits up. We shower in the tight shower stall together. I gently wash her everywhere, and then she returns the favor.

"I love your tattoos," she says as she washes my back. "Especially this one." She squeezes the microphone on my bicep.

"That's the first tattoo I ever got. We all got them together. Our main instrument and the Rebels logo beneath it. We got them the night we signed our first recording contract."

She leans in and kisses my microphone sweetly. "I love that. It's what started it all for you.

After we dry off, I offer her the clothes. "They'll be way too big, but that's all I have."

Her eyes well up with tears. "Seriously?"

Shit. I made her cry. "I'm sorry I don't have anything smaller..."

She interrupts me. "No. I mean it as in you're seriously going to give me clothes to sleep in. No one's ever done anything that nice for me before."

Damn, that sucks for her. I don't know who her last boyfriend was, but he really is a douchebag. "I didn't want you in your concert clothes. That didn't seem like it would be comfortable. Um, do you want to sleep in the empty bunk I promised, or the pull-out in here?"

"If I sleep in here, will you sleep with me?" She pulls on my shirt. As I expected, it's oversized on her, hanging off her shoulders and going to her mid-thigh. And that's one of the smaller, snugger fitting ones on me.

"Absolutely." I wouldn't leave her to sleep in here alone. I usually sleep in just my underwear, but I tug on a t-shirt so she doesn't feel self-conscious wearing one too. I don't want her to feel she has to put her short skirt on just to go to the bathroom.

I'm sure the guys heard us. God knows we've all heard each other at some point. We've all probably heard Killian's women the most. We hear them, not him. He's quiet, which isn't surprising, given his personality.

I make short work of pulling the bed out. Last guy changes the sheets and then folds it back up. That's the bus rules. It's only fair. Then the other sheets get washed when we stop. Our manager has an assistant who's also like a bus housekeeper for us. She straightens up the bus, makes sure our fridge isn't running low on anything. She does our laundry. She's really good. We all leave her an extra twenty dollars every week on top of whatever she makes from the record company. She's a doll and someone we've grown to rely on because she's proven herself trustworthy—a rarity in this business, even with the non-disclosure agreements all employees sign.

I pull the top sheet back as an invitation for Becka to get in, which she does. "Do you want another bottle of water or anything from the front of the bus?"

She shakes her head, but hands me her phone. "Can you charge me?"

I take her phone and plug it in with whoever's charger is in the room. It might honestly just be an extra. Then I crawl in next to her. She immediately curls up with me, using my shoulder as a pillow. She quickly drops off and I soon follow.

Chapter 6

Becka

I startle awake and don't immediately recognize my surroundings. "Sorry. I had to pee." Mavrick Slater from the Blind Rebels is coming back from the small bathroom off the lounge area we've been sleeping in.

"What time is it?" I can't remember where my phone is. I know he's charging it. I probably have to take my pill. I take it every morning at nine. He grabs my phone from the counter near the bathroom.

"It's only 7:24 a.m." He hands me my phone.

"That's oddly specific. Are we still moving?"

Mav shakes his head. "The driver is taking his sleep break. We're parked near a strip mall. Wanna walk over to Walmart? We can get you some clothes that will fit you. And grab breakfast at the diner on the other side?"

I nod. This early, there wouldn't be any other options open to get clothes. When my stomach rumbles, I realize I haven't eaten since lunch yesterday.

Mav chuckles. "Maybe we should hit the diner first, and then the Walmart?" I nod vehemently, and he chuckles some more. "You got it."

After a fairly standard diner breakfast, we head into Walmart.

"I'm sure this isn't your usual clothing store of preference, but I thought we'd get you enough that you have some stuff, so you're not stuck wearing my clothes. Although, I have to say, you totally rock them."

His t-shirt hangs off my shoulder as it's way too big, but I tied it in a knot on one side, which makes it a little shorter before we left the bus. I've pulled his sweatpants up as far as they'll go, and I cuffed them. I'm wearing heels because they're the only shoes I have.

"I look ridiculous, huh?" I can't help my laugh, just imagining myself showing up on that old People of Walmart website.

"You wear my clothes well." Mav winks at me.

I throw my shoulders back for bravado and grab his hand as we enter the store. This rock star is going to fall in love with me. I tried to get Dom to fall for me, but he's obviously a deviant.

He leads us over to women's clothing. "Pick anything you want."

I wander around and pick a couple of shirts and some jeans that will fit me. It's Walmart, so it's cheap stuff, so he can totally afford this. Then he takes me over to the shoe department, and I grab a pair of flip-flops.

"Are you sure you don't want something a little more substantial than flippies?" He glances at the pair I have in my hands. What grown man calls flip-flops flippies?

"Flippies?" I question him.

He shrugs. "Not a very rock star thing to say, is it?"

I can't help the giggle that bubbles out of me while looking at this big, tall, charismatic rock star walking around Walmart, saying things like flippies and randomly trying on things to amuse himself. The best was when he had on a pink furry hat. He didn't even care if someone took a picture of him. I've almost completely forgotten about Dominick, even though it was just last night. So much has happened since then. Good things.

"Can I get some underwear?" I ask him, and his cheeks actually tinge a light pink as he nods. I made Mavrick Slater blush. Who'd have thought that was possible? I grab a three-pack of thongs and he turns even redder.

"Um, is that enough?"

I don't know how to answer his question. "Enough underwear?" My eyebrow raises, and I look between the pack of underwear in my hand and Mav. He nods at me.

"Is there something you're trying to ask me, Mav?" I shoulder bump him as we walk toward the front of the store.

"I like having you around. You wanna stick around a while? Like in a more-than-three-pairs-of-underwear while?"

Jackpot. Step one accomplished: Get a rocker to fall for me. While he hasn't completely fallen, he's starting, and that is exactly what I am aiming for.

He swallows hard, thinking about my underwear, and knowing I'm affecting him this way just walking through a big box store makes me feel powerful.

"The person who does our laundry only does it about once a week, so you might want more. More of everything. As a matter of fact, you stay here and keep shopping. I'll get us a cart."

When he returns, he not only has a cart, but some sort of child's headband with cat ears peeking up from his hair. "What's new, pussycat?" He grins at me. "Find anything good?"

I put my stuff into the basket. "A couple things. Just for now."

"Good. Do you have any favorite foods we should get for the fridge? Are you a yogurt eater?" He gives me a sideways glance, but I'm sure he saw me shudder. "Yeah, me neither, it's sour. Why would anyone want to eat that stuff?"

We run through the toiletries to get me a toothbrush and some other basics. Then he hits his precious snacks. Seems each of the guys likes a different type of snack. He throws a weird conglomerate of goodies into the cart and encourages me to do the same, and I wonder if it's some sort of test. Is he judging me by the type of snack I like?

"Well, what do you like to eat?" I shrug and pick a box of crackers and toss in. "Okay, what about cereal or something? We eat on the bus a lot. So maybe something microwavable? Unless you want to cook. There is an oven and stove, but we never use it for anything more than heating up a frozen pizza. Sammy, he eats a lot. Just to warn you. So we should definitely mark your food with your name on it, or it will go into the bottomless pit we call our drummer. Oh, and do you need to call your friend Kasey and check in with her?"

He seems almost nervous, or worried that I ditched my friend, my life. He doesn't know it was my plan all along, just with someone different. Might as well see where this leads, because I'm not going to lie, the chemistry between us is off the charts. "I'll call her when we get back to the bus."

"You should probably know that Callum's been grumpy lately, ever since I called out his drug use. He's been hitting the coke pretty hard. If you see him using, let me know. He gets crazy as fuck when he's flying high. Last time he tried to jump off a ten-story balcony into the pool, the dumb shit. So just kind of give him a wide berth on the bus, okay?"

I nod again. I learned my lesson about coke. It robbed me of an orgasm and a relationship with Dominick. But it's all in the past now, because I'm pretty sure I'm with who I was supposed to be with all along. Becka Slater has a certain ring to it.

"Got it. Keep my distance from Callum and report to you if I see him doing coke." I flip my head in a tight nod.

"Killian's kind of quiet and stand-offish for the most part so don't be offended if he doesn't say much, and Sammy's friendly so you shouldn't run into any issues with him, but if you do, please let me know. I'll talk to them." Aww, he already cares about me enough to give his bandmates, his best friends, a talking to, should they get inappropriate. I care about him too. We're bonded now.

We walk hand-in-hand, him carrying the Walmart haul that he paid for in his free hand, across the parking lot to the bus and it just feels natural and right. Callum is up when we enter the bus, glaring at Mav over his cup of coffee.

"Um, I'm going to call Kase, okay?" I nod my head toward the lounge area and release Mav's hand.

"Yeah. Good idea. Here, take these with?" He hands me our Walmart bags. When I enter the lounge, I close the doors behind me.

Chapter 7

Mavrick

"You taking over the lounge now?" Callum sneers at me from his coffee. "You have quite the ego these days, Mav." Callum shakes his hair, the front loose, but the majority of his long straight hair is pulled back into a low ponytail at the base of his skull, per usual.

"I had an overnight guest, yes. I don't need your shit. We've all done it at one time or another." I stare him down. I don't know why the fuck he's so surly. Especially toward me. I haven't done a damn thing to him. Except call Jax to get him under control the other night, but this attitude of his, it's been going on for months now.

"Look, man, I don't understand what's going on with you lately. This isn't you. What's up?" I give it to him straight. He's my brother and I'm worried. Neither of us are ones to mince words.

He doesn't say anything. He looks into his coffee cup, swirling it instead of looking at me.

He shrugs. "Nothing."

"You can't bullshit a bullshitter, Cal." I hold my gaze on him, but he still doesn't give me his attention. "Talk to me."

He slams his cup on the kitchenette table. "Leave me alone, Mav."

"No can do, brother. You're not yourself. Coke, man? That's serious shit and you always get crazy on it—"

"Fuck off, Mav!" The vein on the side of his head stands out and his jaw clenches as he hollers.

"You don't want to talk to me? Fine. Whatever. But check yourself. Think of Sammy, if nothing else—if no one else. We lost Sev to drugs. Think of how devastated he'd be right now if you had been successful in your fucking swan dive off my balcony the other night. Think of your brother. Your twin," I growl firmly, our faces nearly nose-to-nose. I want him to hit me, because then at least he cares about something.

The privacy curtain in the hallway flutters. Someone else is up and I don't want to bring attention to anything. "He looks up to you. You're his brother and his father figure. It'd kill him. It'd kill all of us. You get that, right?" I stare into those stormy dark blue eyes and see nothing but anger. At me? At himself? I can't be sure.

I pull back and stand up straight. "If you need something, an ear, a shoulder, say something. If not to me, to anyone else. We're all family here. Now, if you'll excuse me, I have someone else who both wants and deserves my attention." I walk straight through to the lounge, closing the door behind me quietly.

Becka has her phone to her ear, her head tilted as I hear her softly talking to whomever is on the other end. I don't want her to think I'm snooping on her, so I head to the little bathroom and close the door.

Chapter 8

Callum

Mav can fuck off. Asshole.

Like I don't know we lost Sev to drugs. Heroin, to be precise. I was the one talking to the coroner as they took her away from Sammy's condo that day. It was me who worked out where we could afford to bury her because Sammy'd gone into deep debt, trying to clean her up. Trying to save his sister. I'm the one who stood beside Sammy at the funeral, helping hold him upright at the gravesite. So yeah, I think I fucking know we lost Sev to drugs and how it affected Sammy. Killian. And even Mav. It was my fault. I should have been checking in with her.

I don't have a problem with coke. I use it to escape. I use it because I'm tired of being the only one who can take care of every fucking little thing for everyone.

Tired of being the responsible one. Tired of being the fixer. I just want a break. And for a few minutes, coke gives me that escape like nothing else.

Chapter 9

Mavrick

Becka and I spend the rest of the drive snuggling in the sheets, eating buttery, crumbly crackers, and watching some silly sitcom. She seems to like it and that's enough for me. She makes me feel strangely comfortable in a way I'm not used to. Just lying here with her, I feel at home. It's hard to believe I've known her for less than 24 hours.

We finally pull into the venue for the night. The guys all spill out of the bus and go their separate ways before sound check. It's important that we each have our space, even if it's just for a little while. I stay put and pull her tighter to me.

"We'll have a sound check and then some media after. Will you be okay on your own?"

"Sure," she says as she lazily runs her finger over the t-shirt at my abdomen. "I'll play on my phone or something. Should I hang out here? Somewhere else?"

"You can hang out in my dressing room, if you want. Plus, you can get into the green room, where you can grab some food and stuff. Just make sure you stick to the Rebels room, or the other bands might either get cranky or steal you from me." I pull her toward me, already feeling that possessive need for her.

She winks at me. "Do you have to go now?"

"I have a few minutes. Did you have something in mind?"

She grips me around my neck and pulls her face up to mine. "I have a few ideas." Her small hand slithers between my waistband and my stomach.

R

AFTER THE SHOW, the VIP, and the green room bullshit, we climb back on the bus. I peek in the lounge and Becka is sitting up in the bed, reading on a magazine. I recognize it because Callum has one. She smiles up at me and sets her device down. "Good book?"

"I never go anywhere without a magazine." She smiles and sets it down next to her, patting the bed. "So the show was amazing."

I nod. I'd seen her at the side of the stage, swaying and singing along. She looked like she was truly enjoying herself. "Are you sure you weren't bored today?"

She shakes her head. "No way. I had the best time. Seriously. I hung out with this girl, who I guess is your manager's assistant. She was so nice. We had a lot of fun. She made sure I had the right passes and everything so I could enjoy the show. I love watching you guys. I'd do it every night." She turned toward me after I sat on the opposite side of the bed. I love how enthusiastic she is, telling me about her day. "How was the show for you?"

"Oh, it was good. The crowd was on point, per usual." I leave out that I caught Callum fucking a girl in the bathroom ten minutes before we went on. He just fucking disappeared. Someone had to find his ass. That someone was me and an eyeful of his ass is exactly what I got.

"So, the drive tonight will be shorter, and when we stop, it'll be at a hotel. We have tomorrow off. We can hang out and have fun. Unless you have to get home?" I can hear the freaking hope in my own voice. I sound fucking pathetic, but I'm not ready for this girl to leave yet. I'm totally under her spell.

"I'm here until you don't want me with you anymore," she proclaims proudly, crossing her legs and leaning back in the bed.

"You don't have a job or family?" Something I learned a long time ago is that if it sounds too good to be true, it probably is.

She sighs heavily. "I don't have a job right now. I've been living off of my trust that was set up by my great aunt when my parents died. Two years ago, when I turned 23, it got transferred to me. I'm not bragging or anything, but I could live off it for a while if I needed or wanted to. So that's what I've been doing while I figure out what I want to do with myself." She gives me a one-shouldered shrug. "Kasey is my best friend, so she's the only one who would miss me. And she's cool as long as I keep calling her, so she knows I'm alive."

Chapter 10

Callum

"Dude, I feel like we never talk anymore." Mav flops down next to me in the green room. He grabs my shoulder and squeezes tight. "We need to make some music, do some writing. Get this weirdness between us gone. I don't like it. I miss you, brother."

He turns to sit sideways on the couch so he faces me, his long legs crossed. "Seriously, man. What's going on?"

I shrug. "I dunno. I'm tired. We are continuously touring. I'm constantly the father figure within the band, herding and dealing with the three of you. There are always people in my face. Pushy fans, Darren, the media. You." I sigh because by the time everyone gets their piece of Callum, the rock star, there is nothing left of me, for me. "Why can't I let loose a little?"

"Letting loose is fine. Natural and necessary. We all do it. But the coke, man? That's not like you. It's dangerous. I don't want to find my brother dead on the floor of some skanky backstage dressing room or in some hotel room. It would devastate us. You are the heart of this band, Callum."

"Enough of the guilt trip, Mav." I don't want to hear about it.

I'm supposed to be living the rock star lifestyle, hard and fast. That's the way Diminished Capacity lives.

"No guilt, brother, just truths. I don't want to lose another person. We nearly didn't survive losing Sev, and we'd disintegrate if we lost you. I meant what I said. You are the heart of this band, Cal. You always have been." He gazes past my shoulder to the concrete wall beyond the couch, and I wonder if the conversation is over, or if he's just choosing his words wisely.

His eyes snap to mine, serious and dark. "I'm going to lay it out for you, my man. If something happened to you, I don't think Killian would survive it. You know I'd do my fucking best to make sure he did, but mentally, it'd ruin him." He pats my shoulder.

"Just saying." He knows I hate that fucking saying. "No guilt, just some truths to ponder the next time you're thinking of doing blow." He squeezes my shoulder and gets up.

R

I TEAR APART MY ROOM, looking for my black dress shirt. We're going out on the town tonight, and I am on the prowl. I have to get the near-nightly pornographic sounds of Mav and Becka fornicating in the back of the bus out of my head. They go at it every damn night and multiple times, mostly... After sixteen days of it, I need a break.

Of the four of us, I've always been the responsible one. The one keeping the others in line. I went from keeping myself and Killian alive, to caring for myself, Killian, Mavrick, and Sammy.

And for a while, Sammy's sister Sevenya too. Sevenya died right as we were starting to take off.

I can't help but wonder what I missed after she came back from rehab.

She was freshly back from rehab, and Sammy said she was

doing good. We had all just started spreading our wings and getting our own places. Kill lived in a townhouse by the beach in Santa Monica. Sammy moved to a condo close to Killian with his sister. Mav and I shared a huge place off of Laurel Canyon in LA. We sent her off to Bright Horizons in Montana barely three weeks after Sammy got the condo. She was gone over a year, really putting in the work to get and stay clean between rehab and the sober house. She looked so good when she came back.

She died four months later in her bedroom in the condo she shared with her brother. Now Sammy couch surfs between the three of us. He can't bear to be in his own condo, because it's still exactly as it was the day Sev died. I should have been checking in on her myself, not through Sammy. Maybe I would have noticed something was up with Sev.

I'm surprised Killian didn't notice she'd slipped off the wagon—those two were always thick as thieves. He really took to his role as her protector. Being bullied by our mom's various boyfriends and sometimes even our mom, having someone to watch over helped him feel in control. She pulled him out of himself.

Her death rocked the whole band, each member in our own way. But we've stuck together because we are family. And yet somehow, I'm still the unelected, always assumed leader of our crew. You'd think it was Mav, because he's the singer, and the singers are always the charismatic leader type, but Mav would be the first to tell anyone who listened that the leader of this band is me.

I'm tired of being the one who cares. The one who has to keep the others in line. Why can't I fuck girls and leave the next day? Drink until I black out? Do a few lines here and there.

Mav is worried I'm an addict. But I'm not like Sev. Fuck, I'm not. I try to make sure Sammy doesn't see me use. I just like the way it makes me feel for a while. Like I can do everything and be the rock God that I'm deigned to be.

Mav's finally caught a case of the feels, or so he thinks, anyway. I'm pretty sure she's using him. For what, I haven't figured out yet. But I'm keeping a close eye on her. Why? Because his infatuation is making him so blind to what could be happening right under his nose. And I truly think, to her, he's just a celebrity fuck buddy who she can con until she finds the next one. I just hope he doesn't think he's in love.

But I don't care about any of this tonight. Because tonight, I'm looking for someone to bring back to my room. To warm my bed and stick my dick in.

Fuck Mav. I've got game too.

Chapter 11

Mavrick

Today's an off day, and I just wanted to fucking relax for a few hours. Just Becka and me, poolside, her flipping through a magazine under an umbrella in that bright green bikini that she bought herself, but one that I enjoy even more.

But Darren has decided we need to do media today and all that bullshit. Today was supposed to be our fucking off day. To me, a day off means not working. And God knows doing media is work. Droll work, if you ask me.

When we congregate in the hall to make our way to the media room, all four of us are grumpy. Killian, dressed in his black-on-black uniform of sorts, doesn't look happy, but then again, who can really tell when Kill's happy. Sammy's not thrilled but doesn't complain. He does whatever he's asked, for the most part. And Callum is still his surly fucking self. I wish he'd just let one of us know what his beef is. But as far as I know, he's literally kept his nose clean since the little come-to-Jesus meeting we had a few nights ago.

We're split up into groups. Sammy and Killian work the

social media side of the room, while Cal and I are paired to do print and radio.

"So who's the girl you've been cozy with, Mav? All the fans want to know." Dammit. Becka's been hanging around with us for about three weeks now. I should have figured there would be questions about her. I haven't even had a chance to talk to her about it.

"You know me well enough by now, Carla, to realize I don't kiss and tell." I play it off.

"Come on, Mav, give the listeners what they want to know. We asked our audience to let us know what to ask you guys, and over half of our listeners mentioned wanting to know about the girl you've been seeing." She looks over her glasses at me like some kind of kinky librarian. We've been on this satellite radio show many times. And Carla knows us. She knows we don't talk about our private lives. She's getting a bit ballsy. I slap my hands on my thighs, about ready to get up and just walk away, when Cal chimes in.

"Did the listeners mention which of the new songs they like best?" he asks Carla. He's trying to take the heat off me. "The label won't tell us how the new album is doing yet."

"'Burn it Down' seems quite popular," she replies to Cal.

"Ahh, that's a great one. I have a funny story about recording that song. So it was really late, and Mav and Sammy went in search of food, because we were all ravenous from recording most of the day. Once we're in that groove, we work until it's right, until it feels like it's perfect. Anyway, Sam and Mav leave. And Killian and I are sitting there, messing around with our guitars." He smiles, the genuine kind that makes his eyes crinkle ever so slightly, and looks up at her. "So, I stand up to stretch and just rip out a guitar solo. It was so good that Killian stopped what he was doing to watch. We decided that this has to be the solo in 'Burn it Down.' But Mav and Sammy were still out getting food. Turns out, Sammy's battery died, and they were literally stuck in the drive thru at Taco Bell and had been texting me and Kill, asking us to come jump them. But I was too busy, free playing what would become the solo in the middle of 'Burn it Down' to bother with my phone."

"Yeah, I wasn't amused, and neither were the three cars behind us. Thank goodness for roadside assistance," I add. I remember that vividly. We were being honked and cussed at.

Carla seems to let the dating thing go for now. Thank goodness, but I make a mental note to ask Becka her thoughts about situations like this. I'm not giving out her name or anything unless she okays it. It's not something to take lightly—having the media and fans know who you are.

It's a recipe for disaster, and I'll be honest, I really like the bubble we've been living in. The guys won't say shit to anyone. Not publicly.

If there is something they don't like about her, they'd have pulled me aside by now and told me. She seems to get along good with all the guys, even Callum, which is weird, because I get the distinct feeling that he doesn't like her. But when he's face-to-face with her, they get along swimmingly.

When it's time to switch roles, we head over to the part of the conference room with the social media people, and Kill and Sam head over to radio. I bump Cal's shoulder with mine. "Thanks for redirecting back there. I appreciate it."

He nods. "She knows better than to do that." He shakes his head and looks back at Carla with a derisive glare. "That was bullshit. We might want to consider putting her on the media blacklist."

"Good call, man. I'll let Darren know we're not interested in doing stuff with her or her station." I shoot a text to Darren.

In all honesty, the media stuff probably took about two hours. Not bad. I'm still not happy that it was on my day off, but whatever. I head up to our room to change into my boardshorts and head to the pool, where I'm sure Becka is basking in a reclining pool chair under an umbrella.

I stop dead in the short hallway, because Becka is laid out, completely naked, on the bed. Fuck, she's a beautiful sight to behold.

"That's a hello if I've ever seen one." I can't help the growl in my voice.

She grins up at me. "I figured you'd probably head here before the pool. I thought you might want to see what you've been missing today." She runs a finger up her thigh, and my eyes can't help but follow it. I'm surprised I'm not actually drooling.

I'm a lucky fucker because not only is she fun to talk to, and the guys get along with her, but our sex is off the charts. She's perfect.

After a midday romp and some room service, we finally head down to the pool. Killian's in the whirlpool with yet another new woman wrapped around him. Sammy's engaged in a game of Marco Polo with some kids in the pool. Callum's nowhere to be seen. Darren's in a cabana with a few girls, ordering bottle service. He does like to party and schmooze. I am just glad that it's not on our dime.

"Cabana or umbrella?" I glance around the pool and there are plenty of both.

"That umbrella!" She starts us toward the umbrella chair she's picked out. Once she spreads out the towel on her lounge chair, she gets on. I join her on the chair next to her, but I know I don't look as good as she does. Every fucker out here is giving her a once-over.

"Do you want anything to drink? A snack?"

"Get me something fruity and non-alcoholic. It's too hot out here to drink. I'm gonna sit here and either start reading or watch my snack get my drink." She giggles, looking up at me from the bag she's brought to the pool with her.

"I think you'll be the snack later," I growl at her quietly before moving to the poolside bar to get her a fruity virgin colada.

Chapter 12

Callum

Mav moves across the pool area to the bar, leaving Becka sitting under the umbrella. She watches him like she's hungry. I mean, I guess that's a good thing. In the few conversations I've had with her, she seems nice enough, but I can't shake my suspicion of her. My gut screams at me that this relationship isn't right.

She's beautiful, so I don't blame him for going after her. I don't think either of them even noticed me over here, sitting at a table, alone. That's okay. Sometimes it's fun to observe.

Killian's close to, if not already, having sex in the jacuzzi, or whatever it's called. That's nothing new. Our mom broke him. He doesn't trust women because of the shit she did to him when he was younger. And I just had to watch, knowing what she was doing to him was wrong, but not being able to stop it because I was a kid myself. He hid behind the couch most of his childhood, for fuck's sake. I'm not talking about a cute five-year-old playing hide-and-go-seek. I'm talking about a terrified preteen cowering behind the couch while his mother attempted to get him out by nearly pulling out his fucking hair. One specific piece-of-shit boyfriend of hers even pulled a gun on him. He was frozen there, and I had to grab him by the shoulders and walk him out the door.

It's a wonder he's as well-functioning as he is. Him being all brotherly with Sammy's sister helped him grow up. He deemed himself her protector, and protect her, he did. If she wanted to go surfing, he was surfing with her. If she wanted to go to the library, or the second-chance mercantile, he was walking with her. Then she died, and he lost his purpose.

So now he buries himself in whatever woman happens to be handy and willing, and with this lifestyle, there are plenty of them. But he doesn't get close to them. Ever. He even holds us at an arm's length. Even me. And I'm his fucking twin. While we still have the connection to each other we were born with, I hardly feel his true emotions anymore. Seems it started just after Sev died.

Fuck. Sammy lost his sister to a drug overdose, and here I am, dabbling in coke. What the fuck is wrong with me?

He went into massive debt trying to clean her up in private rehabs, when the public ones were a joke. More than once. I still remember him asking if she could come when we suggested that he live with us, as our drummer and our band-mate. He wasn't comfortable leaving her with their mom for some reason. But to look at Sammy today, you'd never know that he lost his sister. He seems like the happiest, and most friendly and well-adjusted of the four of us. And he actually is. I don't know his secret. The world isn't a good enough place for a guy like our Sam.

The chair next to mine scrapes on the patio and a second later, it's filled with Dominick Dynasty from Diminished Capacity. He's wide like a brick shithouse, so he goes nowhere unnoticed, but he doesn't seem to give a damn about anything anyone but booze, drugs, and women, and luckily for him, making music gets him all three.

"You have the oddest crew, Callum. Your bassist is practically humping a chick in the hot tub, your drummer is playing in the pool with kids like he's one of them, and your lead singer is a cocky son of a bitch over at the bar. And you, asshole, are sitting at the pool of our hotel, in jeans and a black t-shirt like a damn creeper." I shrug, but he's not wrong. All four of us are different, but I think that's why we gel so well, both personally and musically.

Pulling something from his pocket, he slaps on the table and slides it over to me. "A little present." He lifts his hand to reveal a baggie of blow. "On the house. Consider it an early birthday present."

Mav would shit a brick if he knew where I was getting my blow. He and Darren have been shaking up the crew since my last escapade, and while they've found a few who have stuff on them, it's usually just enough for themselves. I really shouldn't, especially right now, with the way I am being scrutinized by the guys, but I don't want to be rude. So I slip it into my pocket with a nod of thanks.

"You know I got you covered, man. I haven't seen you in a hot minute, so I thought I'd extend some friendship." Dom's friendship always comes in the form of powder.

When I'm in my right mind, I know that this shit is bad and makes me act like a crazy fucker. But sometimes, being a crazy fucker is exactly what I need to blow off steam. I'm sick of always being the responsible one, so Mav can go fuck himself with his sudden need to be all up in my business just because he's got a case of the feels.

I'll probably just put this away for another day. Somehow, I usually end up in Mav's room, throwing shit off his balcony, whether that be into a pool or a parking lot, I don't give a shit. But he's been shacking up with Becka, and I don't need to scare her with my brand of crazy. Not when I am just starting to get close enough to her to figure out what her angle is with him.

He leans back in his chair and surveys the pool scene. "Is Mav with her?" He points at Becka. I nod.

"Watch her, she's batshit crazy. She went on and on with Bruno, my security dude, about how I was expecting her when I seriously had not seen her before in my life. I finally went out there, and you know, she's hot, so I let her in. We had a few lines and a quick fuck against the wall before a show. She was pissed after and refused to join in with me and Darlene. I was nice about it. I seriously wanted her to join us. Darlene said she did too."

"Um... her name is Darla, even I know that. Why don't you, since you stick your dick in her on the regular?" I can't believe he'd call his quasi-girlfriend by a different name. Sometimes I think he does it on purpose.

He gives me a smug-ass one-shoulder shrug and smirk that tells me he really doesn't care. I knew there was something about Becka I didn't like.

"Anyway, tell your boy he should watch his back with her." I just nod to appease Dom. He did give me some free blow, after all. "I'm serious."

"Okay, I'll tell him. He's been seeing her for nearly a month. I don't think there will be any talking him out of her."

"Then I hope he has a damn good lawyer. I have a sixth sense when it comes to chicks like her. She'll chew him up, spit him out, and tell him that it's all his fault. I think she's a fame whore. Of course, then again, so is Mav. He's so cocky, he probably can't see around his own head to notice she's playing him."

I've had a weird vibe about this chick since he brought her onto the bus, and now, thanks to Dom, my hackles are up about her again. Just when I was starting to think it was my imagination.

"I've been watching her with him. I'll let him know if things seem to go south. Appreciate the heads up, man." I give him the famous bro back slap. This appeases Dom for the time being.

He hangs around and drinks a beer with me, and then wanders away.

Mav's since returned to Becka and seems content to lie next to her under the umbrella while she sips whatever the hell Mav bought her to drink. What the hell game are you playing?

He ventures over to chat with Sammy for a bit, his legs in the pool as he sits on the edge, and she stays reading in the shade. He seems like regular old Mav to me, and she doesn't seem to mind him chatting up our drummer.

I finger the baggie of snow in my pocket and decide maybe it is time I went upstairs for a little Callum party of one.

Chapter 13

Mavrick

"Put the chair down." I approach Cal like he's a scared child, much like I've seen Jax do. "You don't want to do this." I try to shake the water from my hair. I ran up here from the pool because I heard the ruckus from out there. And sure enough, Cal was up here, melting down again. Darren's put him on the parking lot side of the hotel, hoping it would stop his pool shenanigans, but that is not the case. He's damaged two cars, and nearly hit a woman walking past his room, holding her son's hand.

"Fuck you, Mav. Just fuck you. I'm sick of your holier than thou attitude. I'm just being the veritable rock star." He tries to pull off a laid-back, I'm doing what's expected of me vibe. But this senseless destruction is not what's expected of him.

"No, you're throwing stuff out of your damn hotel window. You've damaged two cars and nearly hit a lady and a kid with a chair, dude. At this rate, you're going to owe the record company money instead of getting a nice fat check at the end of this tour."

"Quit being an asshole." He snorts at me with a derisive

look that cuts. I'm trying to talk some sense into his thick head, but he doesn't seem to hear me.

I move a little closer to him. "I wouldn't lie to you about this." I continue my steady approach. "You need to stop acting like a fucking idiot. Pretty soon, there will be no hotels we can stay at. No more money. No more touring. No more Cal." I say the last part quietly because that's the absolute worst-case scenario here.

"Are you trying to kill yourself? Do we need to stop the tour and get you some fucking help?" My words break despite their harshness. "We can get you help, man." He has no response.

The asshole heads toward the balcony with the other chair. He sets it down and peers over the ledge.

"Fuck no, Cal. Stop."

He pulls himself up on the railing, facing the right side of the ledge, and hangs his head. I know he's seen the two destroyed vehicles down there. You can't miss them. One has an office chair still in the middle of its very crinkled hood.

"Callum. Where'd you get the drugs, man?" If he won't stop, I'll talk to his fucking supplier. Fuck, I'd pay the dealer not to sell to Cal, if I knew who he was. "You seemed better. What changed today? And where did you get the fucking coke?"

"Fuck you, Mav. I just wanted to enjoy my off time without you going all shrink on me." He turns to me and walks right up to my face, which he promptly spits in as he talks. "My life is none of your business."

"It is my business. You're my brother and my bandmate; that makes it my business, man. This is not you. You almost hurt a random person walking down there. That's not the Callum I know."

"Maybe he's dead." He looks me in the eye with a challenge.

"You don't mean that."

"Maybe I do." He lifts his chin in defiance and stares at me, his eyes begging for me to challenge him. Callum calmly walks back to the balcony and swings his leg over the railing, locking eyes with me again, and they are set in determination. Fuck if he isn't really going to try to play Superman again.

"Are you really willing to leave Killian alone in this world? Are you going to do that to your twin? For fuck's sake, Cal, please."

He drops his head and blinks, my words hitting a mark somewhere deep inside. He loves his brother, at least, if not himself. Callum then takes a deep breath and turns away from me, swinging his other leg over so now he's perched on the small concrete ledge of his balcony on the wrong side of the rail. I don't know where Jax is, but I couldn't need him more. Fuck me. I continue to move toward him. This time, it's going to have to be up to me to pull him back from the edge.

He stands, hands gripping the rail, and he leans back just a little. Fuck, he's coiling to jump, so I make my move. Taking a deep breath, I spring forward, wrapping my arms under his arms and around his chest, locking my hands together so he'll have a hell of a time getting away. I tug him a few times tight against my chest until he's back to the safe side of the railing. He screeches and flails his arms with the movement, a sign to me that maybe he's not actually trying to kill himself. This is a desperate cry for something, but I don't know what.

I drag him back into his room while he continues to jerk against me, his back to my front. My knees finally give, and we pile onto the floor, me on my back, and Callum on top of me, flailing like an upside-down turtle.

"Fuck. You. Mav." He struggles against me until I finally let go, and he rolls off the top of me.

"No! Fuck you, Callum." When I jump up, he's taken aback by my outburst, but I'm so tired of this scenario replaying itself on this tour. If it hadn't been for finding Becka, I'd think it was cursed.

"I can't do this anymore. I love you. But I don't know how to help you. You're out of fucking control. It's killing me to see you this way."

He watches me rave at him with large, surprised eyes. Not defending himself. No smart-ass comments. Almost like it took this moment to get through his thick skull. I can only hope. But I can't stop my rant.

"Don't try to claim you don't know what I'm talking about. We've been going on tours like this for years, and you've never been like this. You're on some sort of collision course with death, man. I'm seriously starting to think you are trying to kill yourself. Is this some sort of suicidal ideation or whatever the fuck the shrinks call it? The drugs and the crazy stunts? Because something's going to catch you the wrong way, and one of these days, you won't end up on the lucky side, you'll end up fucking dead. Splat on the sidewalk or from an accidental over-dose." I have to throw in accidental, because I still don't think he's purposely trying to kill himself, but for whatever reason, he can't reach out and ask for help. He doesn't feel he can tell us what's going on with him.

Part of me knows this isn't really him right now. He's not in his right mind, so why bother begging him. It's not like he's listening, or he'd have stopped by now. I just wish I was his twin and knew what the fuck was going on between his fuckin' ears.

"I can't be part of your continued decline." I throw up my hands while I turn and walk toward the door. "I'm done, Cal. Done. Come see me if you need to talk or decide you need help or whatever. But I can't be party to this shit anymore."

I feel bad leaving him when he's obviously in the middle of some sort of crisis. But he won't talk and has decided coke is a better therapist than working it out with me like he used to.

We've bounced shit off each other since high school. Why he decided to stop is beyond me. I've done all I can do. I leave him there, blinking at me. And part of me hopes, prays, that this action of leaving will get through to him. Make him see that this isn't the path out from wherever he is.

Killian greets me halfway down the hallway to my room.

"He's okay. We're just a little confused." They do more than just finish each other's sentences. They feel what the other is feeling sometimes. It's kind of unbelievable until you see them in action. It's not something I even bother to question anymore. None of us do.

"He's not fucking okay. He just tried to jump off his own balcony. He was fine when I left him a few minutes ago. But I can't do this anymore, Kill."

"Don't give up on him," his brother begs me quietly, his eyes glancing quickly both up and down the hall to make sure we're alone.

"I don't understand what the fuck is going on. He seems hell-bent on destroying himself. And fuck if he'll talk to me. Do you know what the fuck is in his head?"

Killian looks up at me, his face awash. "Not exactly, no." Here's where I'm in a conundrum; does he really know, and due to bro code isn't telling me, or does he honestly not know what's going on with his brother?

"Do you think he needs rehab? Darren's seriously contemplating it for him."

"I'm almost certain if drugs were pulling him under, I'd feel that pull too. It's how it works for us. If it's something that is all-consuming, like an addiction, I'd feel that pull too." He kicks his Van-clad foot against the hallway wall softly. "This feels confusing." He pulls at his shirt.

"Almost like rebellion? I dunno if it's that, but it's what it feels like to me. Angry rebellion."

"After Sev, I thought he'd know better than to fuck with drugs." Killian turns away, almost as if I slapped his cheek. Besides Sammy, Killian was probably the closest to her. We don't talk about Sammy's sister, Sevenya. Maybe we should. Maybe talking about her would keep Cal straight.

"Fuck!" Callum's scream is slightly muffled but causes Killian's head to snap to his brother's room, and he starts to trot toward that door.

"I'm here for him, for you. To help. I just need to know how," I call after him.

He's having some sort of tangible crisis. I wish he'd just tell me what the fuck is going on with him.

Chapter 14

Becka

Mav's visibly upset when he comes back to the room. His head hangs, eyes squeezed shut as he stands there. And I swear I see tears threatening to break through from behind his lids, the corners dampening. I have to be wrong, though. Why would he cry?

"Mav?" I ask quietly. He says nothing, just slowly shakes his head, his hands fisted next to him.

I'm pulled across the room by his sudden need for me. His need to be comforted is palpable, vibrating right into me. Into my heart that's breaking for him.

I wrap my arms around my rock star and pull him to me, holding him tight like I'm trying to hold him together. His whole body trembles with his silent crying. I lean my head against his as he quietly comes undone.

I don't say anything, since I'm not sure what's upset him. I just pour my love into my touch. I hug him tight. Caressing the back of his head gently, I whisper that I'm here, no matter what's bothering him. I assume it's something to do with Callum, since that's where he rushed off to from the pool, but I'm not certain.

I don't know how long we stand like this, but we do until he breaks his silence.

"I can't do this anymore with him," he says, looking down and away from me. It's as if he's ashamed he's let me see him so emotionally broken. It's then I realize that I'm meant to be here with him.

Mav needs me. He needs someone who's been broken and healed. Someone like me, who can hold him together tight while he comes undone for a little while.

He came to me. He didn't go to Killian, or Sammy or Darren. He came to me.

I don't ask him what he means because, honestly, it doesn't really matter, not to me. Not in the big picture of things.

"I think we might need to stop the tour or something, because he's going to end up dead. I don't know what the fuck to do. He's not himself. He's the exact opposite of the Callum I know. He nearly jumped off his balcony. This isn't the first time. He needs help, and he won't talk to me." He looks up at me, his dark chocolate brown eyes swimming with tears he can't quite seem to shed. It's obviously hard for him to be vulnerable like this. It's hard for anyone, but especially for Mav.

"You love him. He's like a brother. But I can tell you from experience that sometimes people have to want help." He presses his lips together until they disappear into a thin line. "It's hard to watch someone you love go down the wrong path." He nods at my words this time. "But unless he wants to turn around, no one can make him. And pressing him too much might make him run farther away." He drops his forehead to my shoulder.

It's so intimate, him opening himself up like this, and what's more is he's letting me comfort him. This man who plays in front of thousands every night is here with me right now. He's so caring. Just that he's this worried about Callum touches me.

But I can't tell Mav that I've been in Callum's shoes. Forcing him to get help could go incredibly wrong. I know that from experience. I've never brought this facet of myself up with Mav. I don't want him to know that I'm on medication to keep me balanced. I take them in plain sight of him, but I am pretty sure he thinks they are birth control pills.

And it works, for the most part. I still have some bouts, but they are always less intense, as long as I take my medicine every day. I've gone off it once and was thrown into the worst depression of my life. Luckily, Kasey intervened.

Maybe I should talk to Callum. Maybe I can get through to him, plus I can try to test the waters and see if he'd be willing to break the brotherhood bond with Mav. Cal's always been friendly enough to me. Actually, all the Blind Rebels have. And luckily, I've been able to avoid Dominick and the other Diminished Capacity guys. I'm sure I'm a laughingstock to them, and I don't want Mav to be embarrassed by that whole incident between me and Dom.

Mav moves over to the nightstand in our room and pulls out the room service menu. "Is it okay with you if we just order in tonight?" He flips it open and gives it a look before passing the little binder to me.

"That sounds perfect. We can take a shower and cuddle and watch TV."

His lip turns up slightly on one side, and he nods. "That does sound good." When he orders, I go start the shower for him.

We're snuggling in bed, our hair still damp, when room service comes. He insists on answering the door for room service with just his underwear on. I watch the muscles in his back ripple as he reaches for the door, making the eagle tattoo seem like it's flying. I love his tattoos. He only has a few. The eagle on the back of his right shoulder, the microphone, and Rebels logo on his bicep. The small lion on his calf.

And while I've seen a few tats on Sammy, the most tattoos

in the band is a tie between Callum and Killian. Each has a complete sleeve. Callum's is all color work that goes down onto his hands, right to his fingers. He also has a leg tattoo of some sort; I haven't been close enough to him to see what it is, but it's also in color. Killian's tattoos are mostly greyscale, with the occasional purple seven mixed into the work. His sleeve is filled with different images, all entwined in a delicate filigree pattern. Some of it is on his chest and ribs, but the spot over his heart is blank.

I overheard Killian ask Sammy if he should get a black heart there. I think Sammy tried to talk him out of that idea, but who knows if he'll get it or not. It does seem a bit harsh, but would totally feed into how the fans have imagined him into this dark, brooding rock star. Most of the time, I would think they are right in their idolization, but every once in a while, there's something about him where a hurt kid peeks out from behind that stoic mask he wears, and it makes me sad.

I walk our plates over to the tray they left, and then rejoin Mav back in bed, snuggling up tight against him, using his hard, warm chest as my pillow. Mav seems to enjoy snuggling as much as I do, which is not something I'd expect from him. He drops his lips to my head and leaves a kiss on my crown.

"Thank you. For today. Being there." His words are so quiet, I can barely hear them, but I'm thankful I can.

I lean in and kiss his chest over his heart. "Of course. I love you." There. I've said it. I was hoping not to just blurt it out in the throes of passion, but in an intimate moment like this, so it sounds authentic.

He hums onto the top of my head, and the vibration feels good against my skull. "I think I love you too, Becka. I didn't want to, but I do." He snuggles me closer to him.

"You didn't want to?" I glance up at him, one eyebrow raised as I look into those dark chocolate-colored eyes. He nods, his gaze serious.

"My dad wasn't the nicest of guys. He was physically abusive, psychologically cruel, and emotionally unavailable. He never touched me, but with my mom, he was terrible in all ways. I vowed not to love, because I didn't want to bring that kind of pain onto anyone." His eyes glaze over with memories spread thick on them like butter.

I caress his chest with a slow, but purposeful circular motion so he knows he's not alone, that I'm here with him when the images in his heart and his dreams get to be too much.

"But then you happened, right when I least expected it." He looks down at me with awe in his voice.

Rocker one bagged. Now it's just a matter of who to try for next. I'm going to get a song written about me yet.

R

GETTING Callum alone is no easy task. I just want to talk to him. To let him know he's hurting Mav and the other guys. And make sure he realizes who the victims are when he gets crazy. To offer my ear if he wants someone to bounce things off of, to let him know he's not alone when he's depressed or anxious. That there are things you can do for help. Therapy. Medication. Alternative medicine. Meditation. Fuck your best friend's girl.

You just have to experiment with what works right for you. I should know. I've tried them all. Some work, some don't. But I am willing to help him find whatever he needs. But, I just can't get him alone to deliver my message.

I finally get him alone, but it's been weeks. Mav and Callum aren't talking to each other, and there is tension on the bus because of it. Everybody walks around on eggshells. Mav sticks mostly to the back of the bus with me, and Cal sticks mostly to the front, leaving Killian and Sammy lost in between. I considered going for Sammy, but he's a little too soft to be my type.

For this to work, they have to be close, like Mav and Callum. And it's so convenient that I've finally got the opportunity to get Callum alone so that Mav won't be too suspicious.

This morning, I'm in luck. Mav's still sleeping on the bus, and Sammy and Killian are in the little store at the truck stop, stocking up on snacks.

That leaves me and Callum at the coffee shop across the parking lot, at whatever time it is.

"Um, how do you like your coffee?" I ask him as I'm about to order.

"Black," he says gruffly.

"Two coffees, one black, the other with vanilla creamer and lots of candy sprinkles on the top," I ask at the counter. Callum chuckles under his breath.

"Is there something funny about my coffee order?" I ask, blinking up at him.

"Christ, woman, even your midnight coffee order is high maintenance. I must admit, I've been wondering what Mav sees in you. And honestly, what you see in him."

Here is my chance to finally say what I've been rehearsing in my mind all week.

"In him? I see an incredible and strong man, who loves his bandmates fiercely and would do anything for them. He loves them with the kind of family love everyone wishes they had. He loves you like a blood brother. You're lucky you have a blood brother. But Mav and Sammy do not."

His eyes narrow on me, crinkling at the corners, but not in a happy way. "What is this, a one-woman intervention?"

I shake my head vehemently. "No, no, no, not at all. This is me telling you that your bandmates love you. That you mean a lot to them, and they all sense that there is something going on with you and are worried."

He takes a visible step back from me, and his eyes narrow more so that they are just slits.

"Who put you up to this? Was it Mav?"

I shake my head again. "No one did." I sigh and glance around to make sure Mav or the other two haven't joined us. "I see myself in you, Callum. I was diagnosed with depression as a teenager. You can find things that work for you. I have yoga and my meds and reading. Those things keep me balanced so I don't go into those super low lows anymore. But I know what it's like to spiral out of control. To feel like you aren't good enough."

"Look, I don't know what he's told you—"

"Only that he's worried about you. That it's hard on him to see you being careless with your life." I sigh. "I'm just saying that if there is something you need to talk to someone about, you can start with me. Sometimes it's easier to tell a virtual stranger. Sometimes talking to someone with a different vantage point is the best thing. You know where to find me." I reach over and squeeze his arm. "That's all I'll say." I pick up his coffee at the bar and hand it to him.

"Enjoy your coffee." I walk toward the bus. Seed planted. I just hope it grows a connection between him and me like I planned, and this doesn't blow up in my face.

Chapter 15

Callum

Wwhat the fuck was that? An ambush from his fucking girlfriend.

I can't believe that Mav would just unleash his stupid girlfriend on me like that. But at least she's something to look at as she sashays her way back to the bus.

This gives me an idea. Mav thinks he loves her so much. But I need to figure out how true her feelings are for him. And I think I know just the way.

Chapter 16

Mavrick

Callum's pissed at me. Again, or still, I'm not sure. I can't figure out why. Is it because I stopped him from jumping off his balcony? Is it because I told Killian I was done with his shitty behavior? Because it's Thursday?

Usually, we argue about shit or whatever, but once it's out, we're all good. But he's holding shit against me now, and I don't even know what he's beefing with me about. And while it seems he's backed off the coke and partying again, he won't even look at me.

We are at home for a weeklong break before we head back out on the road. I use our band group text, hoping to catch Callum in a good mood.

> Me: Waves look good. Anyone wanna surf?

> Sammy: You know I'm in. Come on, Cal & Kill, let's do it.

There's nothing for awhile.

Sammy: I'm on my way. Can I pick either of you up?

Cal: Fuck you, Mav (middle finger emoji).

Sammy: Come on Cal, let's ride some waves. All four of us, like old times.

Cal: Not interested.

Kill: I'm down. Come on bro.

Kill: Cal?

The three of us surf off the beach at my new Malibu home. I love this place. I have my own entrance right to the beach. Plus, this property is private. Cal's still in the house off Laurel Canyon. He bought me out of my part when I moved.

Becka watches from the beach, sitting there with her ever-present magazine. A vision on the beach, only for me.

Sammy bumps my board with the nose of his. "You like her, huh?"

I nod. "I think she might be the one, Sam."

He slaps my back. "Good for you."

I don't hear anything else from Cal for the rest of the week, and half expect him not to show up to the bus call. But he's there, and like usual, the first one on the bus.

"Hey, man, good to see you." Sammy slaps him on the back. "You good?"

He nods at our drummer as he slings his duffle bag into his normal bunk. He looks up and catches me staring at him, wondering if this leg of the tour will be any different. Wondering if my brother Cal is joining us for the tour, or the crazy motherfucker Callum, who destroys hotel rooms, and then tries to defy death by jumping off balconies.

I don't say anything, instead choosing to break our connections by grabbing Becka's bag and taking it to the back of the bus. I don't ask. I claim. No one says anything. Technically, this leg was supposed to be Killian's turn to sleep in the lounge, but he gladly let me have it. Killian's a solid dude. I think it was his way of apologizing for his erratic-as-fuck brother.

Becka greets all the guys, and everyone is nice to her again, even Callum.

We both stop mid-step when we get to the lounge bedroom. It's been made up like an actual bedroom. The spare instruments and stuff have been put away.

"How did you...?" We both look at each other, speaking at the same time.

"Wait...You didn't?" Again, we talk at the same time.

She stops and giggles. "You didn't do this?" she asks.

I shake my head. "You didn't do it either?" She shakes her head and giggles again.

"We did." All three of my bandmates are standing at the small doorway, straining to see our reactions.

"All three of you?" My eyes land on Callum.

"Yeah," they all repeat.

Well, fuck me running. They all did it.

"We like you and Becka together," Sammy says. "And we want you guys to have the room, so you have space for yourselves, and not just where all our shit lives."

"Sam took out all his clothes. Cal and I moved all the extra instruments into the first bunk. We made a rack and organized them and everything." Killian glances at his brother, who simply shrugs.

Callum doesn't say anything to me. I don't say anything to him. The unspoken tension is still so thick in the air, Sammy fidgets, feeling it and not knowing how to approach it.

"Well, I love it!" Becka squeals. "Thank you! All of you." She gives each of the members a hug and a personal thank you, but lingers slightly longer with Callum, as if she's trying to soothe the tension between him and I.

The bus gets underway, and Becka stretches out on the bed, which now has a bedspread instead of just a blanket.

"I think they even added a pillow topper to the pull-out. Come sit with me, Mav. I swear it's softer." She pats the bed next to her.

I sit down with her, and she's right, it does feel softer. I take her hand and kiss it. I think I'm going to ask her to marry me. It seems crazy, even to me. I've only known her for three months. But I love this girl. She gets me.

"I gotta write with the guys today. We should have started during the off week, if we're to get the new album out."

Chapter 17

Becka

I love being on tour with the Blind Rebels. I get to see parts of the states that I probably wouldn't have ever seen if not for traveling with the band. I'm treated like royalty by the crew. I stand at the side of the stage and watch the shows. I know everyone backstage, and they know and love me because they know I'm with Mav. I love that adoration. Totally what I was looking for. And Mav watches for me when he's onstage. I love that too.

On the bus, they've been working on music. Usually, I stick to the bedroom, because I don't want to interrupt or distract them, but I love listening to them work on the music, so I crack the door so I can listen in. Being the first person who gets to hear their newest music is so cool. I'm so fucking lucky. It's a bonus for me.

Today, we break for lunch while the driver sleeps, and we all head to a nearby restaurant. The band walking in causes quite the scene in this poor little unsuspecting restaurant. They put us in a back room, but people kept trying to get to the guys. Jax, their head of security, has one other guard with him, working on the chaos while we eat.

83

Mav and I lag back in the restaurant so Jax and the other guard can walk the rest of the Rebels to the bus.

"They'll be back for us. But before they come back... I wanted to talk to you." His voice is deep and so serious, it makes my stomach flip-flop.

I turn to face him fully, worried about his suddenly serious tone. Why this sudden weird need to talk?

"Babe. Becka. I love you. Will you marry me?" He pulls a ring out of his pocket. It's a beautiful ring, and I'm nodding before I can say yes. Rocker locked down. Heck yeah.

"Yes? Say it so I can hear it," he demands playfully. I'm so excited that he's asked me. I think I really love him. But at the very least, I'm getting my one-way ticket out of my life and into the glitz and glamor of Los Angeles.

"Yes, Mav. Of course. Yes!" He leans in and kisses me, his mouth sweet against mine. I want to kiss him back, but my brain is in overdrive. Oh my goodness, Mav just asked me to marry him! Kase is going to flip out. I can't wait to tell her. He slips the ring on my finger, and it's way too big, but I don't care. I love it.

"We'll take it to get it sized. I promise." He kisses my hand next to the too-big ring, and then works his way up my arm. "I love you, Becka."

"Hmmm, I love you too, Mavrick Slater." I wish we were anywhere but here in this restaurant's back room. When he gets to my neck, he nibbles across to the other side, and then hits that sensitive spot behind my ear, humming as he goes, and the vibration makes me wet. Finally, his lips crash against mine and our tongues tangle.

"Let's go, Mav, Becka." When Jax says it's time to move, it's time to move. But Mav grabs my hand tight and looks over at me and grins so widely, and I'm sure my grin back is just as wide.

"Are we keeping this a secret, or is it something I can tell

Kasey?" I ask as we're escorted back to the bus at a brisk pace. "I'm willing to tell the world, if you are." The smoldering look he gives me at my words turns my insides to jelly.

"Oh, heck yeah! We're getting married!" His loud announcement echoes through the parking lot, and a few people shout their congratulations. I can't tell if they are fans who have been milling about because word got out that the Rebels were stopped here, or if they are just shoppers, but it makes it all the more special.

I follow Mav onto the bus, and I'm not even all the way in yet when he announces our engagement.

"I'm officially off the market!" The guys all turn in unison to look at us, so I hold up my ringed finger. The ring's so big it sloshes on my finger when I do, but I don't want to take it off.

"Congrats, man!" Sammy bounds up from his seat and hugs Mav in that brotherly way, and then hugs me. "A beautiful ring for a beautiful girl."

But as soon as Sammy lets me go, Callum jumps up and gives me a long look that I can't get out of my head before sequestering himself in the bathroom. There was nothing happy about his reaction at all. So now Killian just stands between us and the bathroom awkwardly, kind of stuck in between.

"Sorry. Congrats, man," he says quietly, averting his eyes from us both. It's the most words I've heard him say since I've been on the tour with them,

"I appreciate it, Kill." Mav man-slaps him on the back as he walks us back past the bathroom, giving the bathroom door a hard kick before he leads me into the lounge, which I guess is now our bedroom.

"Sorry about Callum being a continual asshole. He never used to be this way. I'd be fucking happy for him, if the roles were reversed. I don't know what his deal is with me lately. I think we're good and something like this happens. But it doesn't matter. The only thing that does is that I love you." He kisses me as he shuts the door behind him.

As our mouths melt, I can only wonder how true it is that Mav would be happy for Cal and me if he found out about us. While I don't have Cal's ring on my finger, I've had his cock inside me multiple times.

Chapter 18

Callum

Just fucking great. It was bad enough he was dating her. Now he's announcing to everyone and their fucking brother that he's marrying her.

I wish he had at least mentioned it to me before he proposed. I have some major issues with Becka and Mav being engaged, but nothing I can give words to now, especially to him. But maybe if Mav and I talked about it before, I'd figure out how to give it a voice. I'm not going to look like the biggest asshole in the world in front of everybody on the bus.

Especially in front of her.

If he knew about us, he'd kill me, and honestly, he probably should.

What the fuck is wrong with me? It's got to be the coke. She made the first moves, but I didn't have to cave into her. I told myself it was for the greater good. That I was testing her allegiance to Mav. That might've explained it if it was just once. If I had brought it to him right away. But it hasn't been just once, and it's been going on between us for weeks.

She's made it clear to me that her heart belongs to Mav, but that he's too gentle, too nice with her. That I satisfy an itch for her, so to speak.

This only makes me wish I had some blow, so I could numb out and not think about it. What the hell is wrong with me? If I were in my right mind and not coked out more than I'm not, I wouldn't be in this situation.

I'm not stupid enough to bring any blow onto the bus. And I'm definitely not going to do it on the bus. What if I did it and went crazy like Mav says I do. What if Sammy saw?

I could hurt one of the three people who mean the most to me in the world.

But haven't you already done that?

It's bad enough I couldn't help keep Sevenya clean. That I didn't recognize she was as troubled as she was. If only I'd have realized she was using again. Maybe I could have stopped what happened to her. I wouldn't have had to console her brother while we waited for the medical examiner. Killian wouldn't be as dark, as silent as he is. Mav wouldn't be about to marry the very person I fucked six hours ago. But none of this explains the depth to which I've descended. There's no way to get out of this, and that just makes the song of cocaine even sweeter.

Chapter 19

Mavrick

I'm so ready for this tour to be over. It's been especially sucktacular with Callum's attitude problems. Cal and Becka seemed to be getting along, but since I've announced our engagement, Callum doesn't seem to like Becka. Or me. Or our relationship.

He's had plenty of chances to say something about it to me, but has he? No. Instead, he throws a hissy fit in front of everyone when I announce our engagement. He's been a confusing mix of hot and cold lately, and I just don't get it.

At least her friend Kasey was happy for us. I can't wait to meet Kasey officially. The first time we met, it was an awkward exchange of me giving her Becka's keys, but Becka raves about how much she misses her and how good of a friend she is. I'm glad Becka has someone like that in her life. I used to—it was Callum. But now? I'm beginning to wonder if the Rebels have reached their end.

With the way Becka talks about Kasey, I feel like I already know her. And listening to her tell Kasey about our engagement makes me happy.

She shows Kasey the ring over FaceTime. "It's a little too big

right now, but isn't it beautiful? I love him so, so much, Kase."
My heart squeezes at hearing her gush about the ring and me,
and her friend's squeals of delight almost make me blush.

"I'm so happy for you, Becka. He treats you right and makes
you happy. That's all that matters to me," she tells my girl.

I'm antsy for this conversation to be over, so that I can make
love to my girl. My fiancée.

My girl.

That sounds weird, even to me, and I just proposed to her,
but fiancée sounds even weirder. I used to worry that I'd be like
my dad and have a propensity to harm women, but Becka's
shown me that's not who I am. I can love a girl and treat her
right.

"You have that silly love-sick puppy dog look to you that I
love." Becks wraps her arms around me and rests her head on
my chest for a few minutes before looking up at me. "What
were you thinking about?"

I can feel the blush really hit my cheeks now; it's not something I do often. "You. How much I love you. You put the dopey
love-sick look on my face every time."

"Well, it's a good look on you." She reaches up on her toes
and kisses the end of my nose. "Thank you for this." She waves
her hand at me. "This ring is perfect. I would have picked out
the same one."

"You don't think this is too fast? I was worried you'd think I
was moving too fast." I mean, we've only known each other for
four months.

"When does love have a time limit, Mav? Sometimes love
comes fast and people know they are with their soulmate
within days or even hours. Sometimes it takes many years. I
think it depends on the couple. And this is our perfect timing.
We've spent a lot of time together, like close together. Most
couples don't start out that way. We are just lucky." She kisses

my nose again, but this time, she runs her hands up my shirt, lightly scraping me with her nails as she goes.

"Hmmm, lift your arms." She does as she's told, and I rid her of the Blind Rebels crew t-shirt she talked one of our tour guys out of. "Good girl."

I release her gorgeous tits and caress them, enjoying the full weight in my palms. If there is one thing I know, it's that she loves her tits being played with, and I am the guy for that.

"So perfect," I tell her as she thrusts them harder into my hands with a deep moan. I stop only long enough to pull my shirt off and rid myself of my pants.

She bends over in front of me as she does the same. I can't help but stand behind her, and when she stands, I pull her to me. Walking her so she's sandwiched between me and the wall, I use my leg to move hers apart.

"Mav!" She flails her hands back toward me, trying to grab at my hips, then pushes back into me. "Please!"

I reach up and rub those tits again, so she drops her hand, trying to touch herself.

"Nope." I remove her hand and put it up on the wall. Then do the same with the other one. "Hands stay up here."

"But—"

"No buts. Hands stay up here. Or I'll hold them up here. And if I have to do that, I can't do this." I palm her nipples, and then give them a slight pinch, just like she loves.

"Are you ready? Can you keep your hands on the wall?" She nods and undulates her hips with another moan. I grab her hips and push in against her, slow but steady, as she pushes back.

"Oooh, Mav..." She carries the 'v' in my name out as I reach the hilt, and she tips her hips back toward me.

I start off sawing in and out, nice and slow, trying to keep myself under control, but she keeps trying to get me to pick up the pace. Finally, I reach around her and give her breasts another squeeze.

She looks back at me. "Quit teasing me." Pressing back against me hard, she squeezes me inside. "Just fuck me already."

"As you wish, fiancée." I move her so she's facing the arm of the couch, even though the bed is pulled out. She knows exactly what I want and bends over the arm, pushing her ass up in the air. I slide back in, and she pushes up against me, hugging a pillow to her chest.

"Mav! Yes!" I get us into the rhythm I know she loves, and she builds quickly. She's so fucking responsive to me.

"So. Close." She starts to squeeze me tighter, so I pull out and lean over her back to lick it from the base of her spine to her neck.

"No. Don't you fucking stop," she whispers hoarsely as she pushes up against me. "Ugh. Dammit. Mav. Please." She undulates and grinds against me harder. I lightly run my pointer fingers around each nipple, and she presses her chest forward and her ass out at the same time.

"Are you sure you're ready?" I whisper in her ear.

"Please, ugh." I give her exactly what she wants, hard and fast. Her skin glistens as I build her back up again.

"Shit!" She bites the pillow and stiffens as she convulses around my length. I pull out as soon as I can and squeeze myself as I watch her. I'm not quite done with her yet.

"I love watching you come, Becks. But it's my turn."

She nods and rolls onto her back on the bed, panting from her orgasm.

"Okay." She lets her legs fall apart and nods, so I know she's ready. She's super sensitive right now, and I guide her legs over my hips as I line myself up, careful not to put any pressure on her clit. Then I penetrate her.

After a few slow pumps inside her, she's meeting me halfway. I'm just about to go off when she circles her hips and grabs her breasts. The sight of her kneading her own breasts makes me jealous, and I pull her hand off one so I can give it a lick and a tug with my mouth. She moans and pushes it toward me as I thrust.

"Shit!" My balls tingle, and then tighten as I come.

"Wow, that was...the shit," she pants as I move to collapse next to her on the bed.

A few hours later, there's a knock on the door. It's probably at least three in the morning.

"Mav, we're here." Sammy taps his drumsticks on the door.

"Oh... kay!" I stutter as Becka wraps her hand around my dick and squeezes as she sucks on my neck. "We'll be out in a bit!" I try to keep my voice even as the minx keeps pumping me in her hand as Sammy retreats, surely knowing what's going on.

"Oh, Becks," I groan and lift my hips as she continues to work me. "Fuck. So good." She squeezes hard, and then bends down and sucks me into her mouth.

She works her tongue around the underside as she sucks, and I'm going off like a geyser in seconds.

"Fuck. Damn, I love waking up like that."

She giggles in that lighthearted way that I adore. "I love it when I surprise you. Your eyes get all bugged out like you can't believe what's happening, but you don't stop."

"Of course, I don't stop!" I grab her and tickle her, just to watch her squirm. "I guess we best get dressed and check into our room for the weekend."

Chapter 20

Becka

Touring is getting boring. Mav and the guys have a lot of media on this leg and don't always take me along with them.

Today, they are doing media somewhere in the hotel, at least. That usually means that Mav will come find me in the room or by the pool and we'll go out if he doesn't have to go right to the arena.

There's no show tonight and we've been planning to go out together to a club. I'm so excited to go out on the town.

"Hey, you! I miss you. How is life on the road?" Kasey smiles from my phone screen.

"I'm so bored. Mav's doing media. Again. It's, like, almost every time now. But at least we have a nice hotel. This one has a fancy restaurant. Normally, they are like three-star type places, but this one is solid 4.5 stars. Don't get me wrong. Anything is better than life in Chicago."

"Sounds nice to me. All that traveling. I guess it worked out for you, even if it didn't work out with Dom." She flips her hair. "You're engaged to a rock star! How cool is that? I mean, that's what you always wanted. You just thought it would be with Dom."

"I can't believe I ever liked him. He's such a dick. Mav is a way better singer. Plus, I think Mav's just a better person."

"Then there's Callum..." Do I dare tell Kasey? I don't know that she'd understand why I get with Callum on the regular. That having one rock star is good. But having his best friend too is even better.

"What do you mean?" I can hear the question in her voice, and I know she's not ready to know about Callum and me yet.

"He's worried about his best friend. And when he's worried about him, it means he's not paying attention to me. Not the right kind, anyway. Maybe I can help with Callum."

"Maybe he's jealous of Mav?" She flips her hair again, and it flashes across my phone's screen.

"No, I don't think that's it."

"How are you going to find out, though?"

"I dunno, Kase, maybe I can pull Callum aside tonight when we're all out. Did I mention that? We are all going out together to a club. It's going to be so fun." Better to get Kasey's mind off of Callum before she figures it all out.

"Sounds fun. I miss hanging out with you. I miss our gang going out together. Are you sure you should be pulling Callum aside, though?" I don't understand why Kasey can't let the thing about Callum go.

"I'll only do it if I can get Mav distracted with something else."

"Oh, okay. I miss you. When are you coming back?"

"The whole idea is to not come back... but don't worry, Kase. Mav's place has plenty of room. He has more bedrooms than he knows what to do with. He actually said that. Sammy even has his own room there. I'll ask Mav if you can move in with us. Maybe you can hook up with Sammy or something. I'd say Killian, because I know you like them dark and broody, but he's always with someone. A different someone each time. I think you're better off with Sammy. Wouldn't that be cool?"

She shrugs. "I dunno, moving to Los Angeles seems scary. Especially with no job or no way to support myself."

"I don't have a job and I'm moving there. Mav doesn't mind. He asked me to marry him, after all."

There's a noise at the door, and it sounds like Mav might be done. "I have to go. I'll call you later!" I hang up on Kasey just as Mav comes through the door, muttering to himself.

"How was media?" I ask as he flings his phone and keycard onto the dresser.

"Ugh. I hate it." He doesn't look up at me. I can tell he's in a bad mood. Maybe going shopping will cheer him up like it cheers me up.

"Let's go shopping. I'd love a new outfit to wear tonight." I've been looking forward to us all going out. It's been planned for almost a week, which in tour time is forever, I've learned.

"I really don't want to go out. Shopping or tonight." He flops onto the giant armchair in the corner of our room and looks wistfully out our window.

"But I've been looking forward to this all week." My lip sticks out like a petulant teenager. I'm sick of hotel rooms, even when I'm not alone.

"So then go," he snaps at me as he removes his boots, putting his feet on the small coffee table.

Wow. I blink several times, not believing he's talking to me like this. But I can work with this. This is exactly how I'll get Callum alone again.

"Is that really what you want, Mav? Your fiancée going out to a club alone at night?"

"For fuck's sake, Becka, quit being so damn dramatic. You wouldn't be alone. You'd be with the band. If you want to go, fucking go. Here..." He rifles through his wallet and flips his black credit card toward me, it landing on the bed between us.

"Knock yourself out. But I'm not going shopping, and I'm not going clubbing."

"Fine!" I snatch the card from the bed, grab my purse, and leave. Fuck him if he doesn't want to be with me. I'll make him pay, quite literally. I think I might need more than just a new outfit.

Chapter 21

Becka

After a few hours of retail therapy and a mani-pedi at a salon, there's no word from Mavrick. I ride share back to the hotel, thanking the driver and making sure to tip him well with Mav's card that I now have saved into my phone. While I wait at the elevator, someone steps up right behind me and whispers in my ear.

"Hey." Callum. I recognize the grit in that voice anywhere.

He laughs. "Are you sure you want to settle in with Mav and not me?" He's so close to me, I can smell the leather of his jacket, and it instantly has me pressing my thighs together.

He chuckles quietly, and my stomach quivers in anticipation. I want him to touch me right here in clear view of everyone, but if he did, Mav would find out within minutes, I'm sure.

I rush into the elevator as soon as the doors open, and he joins me. Callum seems to fill the small space.

"I wanted to thank you for offering your ear and other things...I've been enjoying. It was rude of me not to thank you." Callum's tongue darts out and wets his lips as he looks at me. His eyes are a dark stormy blue color that I could get lost in.

He flicks one of the shopping bags, trying to get a reaction out of me. Little does he know, my body's reacting plenty. The floors count off with a beep as we pass each one, and I swear the dings are getting further apart.

"You got something cute and frilly you can wear for me instead of Mav in there?" His eyes sparkle, and he leans in close to me. I can feel his warm breath, and my heart thunders in my chest. I want Callum to kiss me, touch me without the reverence Mav touches me with. What about Mav? If he finds out, my move to LA is off.

Finally, the elevator stops, and I can't get out of it fast enough as he chuckles and saunters out behind me, but stops at the door to his room. Thank goodness, because we can't get caught. It would implode the band, I have no doubt, and then I'd never get to Los Angeles permanently and songs won't be written about me. Or at least not the kinds I want written.

I fumble with my card at the door, but when I get in, Mav isn't here. I check the credenza and end tables for a note. Nope. Nothing on my phone either. I don't know where he is. But he told me to go if I wanted to go, so I change into one of my new outfits, stopping to admire the amazing job the girl at the salon did on my nails. Sparkling red, with BR drawn artfully on the nail of the ring finger.

There's a knock on the door. It can't be Mav, or he'd just walk right in. "Hey, you guys ready?" Sammy bounces on the balls of his feet as I open the door. He's wearing dark jeans and a dark blue button-up shirt. It's the first time I've seen him wear anything other than shorts.

"I am. Mav's not coming." I grab my new bag and pull the door shut quickly behind me.

"Oh?" He looks up at me, puzzled.

I shrug. "He's in a mood."

We meet the twins in the lobby. Both are wearing black leather pants. Callum wears a dark green button-up shirt with a darker green pattern. Killian wears a worn, ripped, black band t-shirt and a leather jacket.

"Mav?" Killian asks, eyeing his brother.

I shake my head. "He came back from media in a bad mood. Didn't want to go shopping with me. Told me to go by myself if I wanted. Wasn't even there when I came back from getting my nails done." I frown and shrug.

"Where is he?" It's the first Callum's spoken to me since our encounter in the elevator. He looks good though. Without Mav here it might be easier to slip off one at a time and rendezvous.

"Not sure. He didn't leave me a note or text me or anything."

Now it's Callum's turn to frown. Mav's disappearance seems to have put a damper on the mood in the limo taking us to the club. Everyone's quiet. Callum glances at me quickly before he looks out the window, while Killian and Sammy both mess around on their phones. I feel like the fourth wheel here. It's awkward, and I shouldn't have come without Mav, but it's too late now.

We're escorted into the club as a group by Jax and two other security guys through a back door. Jax seems to know his way and marches us right to a separate VIP area with several couches and comfy chairs on the edge of the dance floor. We can hear and see everything, and we have bottle service here.

A waitress in a skimpy dress and heels higher than mine comes up and takes drink orders. I order a rum punch, but I don't think she's heard me. She's too busy fawning over Callum, Killian, and Sammy to even notice me.

"Um, excuse me, did you get hers?" Sammy motions to me.

"Oh yeah, a rum and coke, right?" She smiles, and I can't tell if she's purposely getting my order wrong or if she's just a star-struck moron.

"No, a rum punch, please." She nods and heads off toward the bar.

"Thanks, Sammy." He smiles at me. Looking around, I don't want to just sit in the VIP. "Do you want to dance?"

"Um, sure. I'm not that good." He shrugs and stands, offering me his hand, but the waitress is already back with our drinks and starts passing them around.

"That's okay. Neither am I, but I promised myself I'd come out and have fun, with or without Mav." Sammy nods like he agrees with me.

I sip my drink. Bleck, I force myself to swallow. It's a rum and coke. Stupid cunt.

"It's okay to leave your drink. Jax and the guys will watch it." He guides me to the dance floor. Sammy's not shy at all and that brings out the extrovert in me.

We giggle and dance until we're both ready to take a break and have something to drink. When we get back, Callum's disappeared. Killian's got a girl on his lap. And my drink looks exactly like I left it.

I take another timid sip, trying not to make a face.

"Don't like your drink?" Sammy asks as he tips back a sip of his beer.

I shake my head. "She gave me a rum and coke anyway." I sigh. "I don't want to waste it. I'm not even sure how much it costs."

"You don't have to worry. Drinks tonight are on Monumentus. Our record company."

"So I can order something else?"

He giggles and hails our cunt of a waitress back over. "Life is too short to drink shit you don't like."

After my new drink comes, an actual rum punch this time, I excuse myself to the restroom. When I return, Sammy's ready to hit the dance floor some more, none the wiser.

We have a lot of fun. He's pretty good, actually. Typical drummer. Their heads just work differently, and they can understand complex beats and anticipate the next move.

101

We're having yet another run on the dance floor when Sammy stops dancing suddenly, leaving me to bounce off of him as he stands there like a statue.

"Shit. Uh, sorry, Becka. Go to the VIP area and tell Jax we have a Callum situation by the stage." Sam starts toward the stage, and I glance that way, noticing Callum climbing a light scaffolding.

I rush right up to Jax, who catches me by the biceps lightly. I've never said more than a quick 'hi' or 'thanks' to him before, and he is slightly intimidating. "Sammy says there is a Callum situation at stage right." I point out Callum, and he rushes out of the VIP area.

"What's going on?" Killian is next to me before I can even find Jax in the crowd.

"Your brother is going crazy again." I point to the scaffolding, where Callum now hangs half off, shouting at the crowd below him, but I can't hear him over the music.

"Fuck. Stay here." He rushes off in the same direction as Jax and Sammy. Soon Jax has made short order of the scaffolding and somehow convinces Callum to come down. He marches Callum back to the VIP area with Killian and Sammy quick on their tails.

"You!" Callum slurs at me. "You were practically humping Sammy." Shit. Callum's eyes narrow in on me and I can read the unsaid accusations in his eyes. *When he was just in me. And was he.*

"I wasn't humping Sammy. We were dancing." What's gotten into him? He knows better than to air this in front of others. We agreed. Our secret rendezvous need to stay secret.

Killian jumps between me and his brother, facing me. "I'm sorry. He must have taken something. He doesn't know or mean what he says." He turns back to his brother. "Quit being a dick. Let's go. Party's over." He pushes Callum toward the back door, the same one we came in through, Jax following.

Sammy and I are escorted out a few minutes later by one of the other security guards and take a seat across from the brothers.

"You're freaking me out, Cal." Killian's voice sounds more like an upset child than the adult he is as he talks to his brother softly. It's definitely not his usual voice. "What's going on with you?"

"So, you're a good dancer. Mav sure missed out." Sammy is purposely trying to distract me to give the twins privacy in the back of the large limo.

"Thanks. I took ballet for a few years when I was a kid. But no formal training or anything. I just like to dance." I shrug. Sammy engages me in small talk the rest of the ride back to the hotel.

Sammy and one of the security guys walk me to the room I share with Mav. I have no idea if he's here or not. "Thanks for walking me to my room. Thanks for dancing with me too. Goodnight, Sammy."

Chapter 22

Becka

"Night, Becka!" Sammy watches me enter my room, and I assume he and the security guard leave for his room on the other end of the floor.

"There you are. Have fun publicly humping my drummer?" Mav sneers from the chair he was in before I went shopping. On the table in front of him is a glass half-filled with an amber liquid that's too light to be a coke.

"Sammy danced with me because you weren't there to dance with. And yes, I did have fun."

He waves his phone at me. "Callum ratted you out."

"You're trusting Callum now? The same Callum who got so whacked out on something that he climbed the scaffolding at the club and had to be removed forcefully by his own bodyguard. That Callum?" I slip off my heels, holding one in my hand. If he pisses me off any further, he might be wearing one of them on his head.

"Whatever." He grabs his drink and gazes back out the window.

"Whatever? You aren't even the least bit worried that your

friend, your purported brother, is obviously crying out for help? He could have killed himself tonight."

"What do you care about Callum?" He doesn't understand that I care about Callum because, well, because he's a good guy. He's a little messed up right now. But I understand where he's coming from, and it doesn't seem that Mav does right now.

"I care about him because you care about him. Just like I care about Killian and Sammy too."

He huffs and empties his glass.

"Why did you bug out on me? You're supposed to be my fiancé. It was embarrassing to have to tell the guys I didn't know where you were."

"I told you; I didn't feel like going out." He doesn't even get up from his seat, just continues gazing out of the sliding glass doors.

"If you didn't feel like going out, where were you when I got back from shopping?"

He just grunts and won't even look at me.

"Mav, did you sleep with someone else?" I don't want to think he did that to me. We are engaged. But I can't help but think of Dom and Darla.

"No, I didn't sleep with someone else. Don't be ridiculous, Becka." He rolls his eyes.

"Then where were you when I got back from the shopping trip that you forced me to go on alone?" I keep seeing Dom thrusting into Darla.

"I didn't force you to go anywhere. You decided to go shopping. You decided to go out to the club without me." He stands from the couch.

"Because you were₁ here." I don't know how to spell it out for him any easier.

He throws his empty glass, and I can't help but jerk in surprise when it smashes against the wall and shatters.

"You're drunk. Sammy's room is down the hall, 1245. Go

sleep it off." I point toward the door and stomp my foot. I'm not sleeping in the same room as him if he's going to act this way.

"This is my room. My name is on it. Not yours." His lips are pinched so tight they're white and his fists ball up.

"If you don't go sleep it off at Sammy's, I will." I arch my eyebrow and cross my arms, taking my stand. But instead of really going to Sammy's, I'd probably go hang with Callum instead. He's usually horniest when he's wacked out, and I could really go for a quick Callum-bang against the wall.

"Fuck, you're a bitch tonight," he spits in anger.

"And you're a drunk asshole." I start to systematically pack my things to take them down the hall to Callum's room. I know he'd more than let me sleep in his room.

"Fine." Mav grabs his keycard and his shoes and takes off down the hall.

A while later, while I'm snuggling down in bed, I get a text from Sammy.

> Sammy: Mav's out like a light. Good call sending him my way. Sorry he's being an ass. If you ever want out, come to me. I'll get you home.

Chapter 23

Mavrick

My head throbs rhythmically, and I'm afraid to open my eyes. I have a feeling the sun will burn the retinas right out of my eyeballs if I open them. Then I hear something beating to the same rhythm as my head and risk a peek. Sammy is sitting in the chair with a pillow in his lap, drumming the fuck out of the pillow with a pair of drumsticks.

"Sam," I rasp. "For the love of Jim and Jack, please stop."

"Sweet. You're finally awake." He joins me on the bed and starts bouncing it, the motion threatening to expel the contents of my stomach.

"Sam. Stop. I'm gonna chuck."

He abruptly stops the hideous bouncing motion. "Don't you think you should probably get up and apologize to your fiancée?" Sam tips his head at me. "Fiancée, Mav. You were a fucking dick to her yesterday. She had to shop by herself. She came out with us by herself, and then you pissed her off so bad, she threw your drunk ass out of your own hotel room."

"Fuck." I did do all of that. I knew I'd end up fucking this up. Fucking up must be in my genes.

"I highly suggest groveling, if you want to keep her." Eyebrows raising, he purses his lips.

He sighs and looks hard at me. "Just so you know, last night, I let her know if you ever fuck things up beyond all repair, she can come to me. I'd make sure to get her home safely. So, she might already have one foot out the door, man. And if I did something to cause that, I'm sorry."

We don't deserve Sammy. He's always been more of a lover than a fighter. He hates conflict and is always trying to smooth things over between us when we have disagreements. But it's more than that. He's more than that. He's always looking out for everyone. He's probably more worried about Callum than I am, but because he doesn't want the conflict, he doesn't say anything.

"Thanks, man. I appreciate you looking out for her. It means a lot."

I pause, wondering if I should bring up Cal, but I do it anyway. We can't keep ignoring this, hoping it fixes itself, or he'll end up dead. "Can we talk about Cal?"

The corners of Sammy's mouth pull down and he nods, kicking his foot against the nightstand next to the bed. "I'm worried about him too."

"I think he's self-medicating, but the question is why?" Sammy knows a little something about self-medicating since he found his sister's diary after she overdosed. I hate that this thing with Callum might bring up some other shit for Sammy, but I need to talk to someone, and I don't feel comfortable sharing it with Killian.

"I'm beginning to worry he's half-assed suicidal. It's like he purposely does this shit, but only when someone is around to stop him. And we always do. But one of these days, we're going to be too late. Or he'll get some coke cut with something bad and he'll OD. I don't know what to do."

Sammy seems to consider what I've said. "And what the hell

is with all the jumping off things? It was bad enough with balconies, but now a lighting scaffolding? Do we have to worry about him during our shows now? We use similar ones. That's all we need, for him to do that shit and misstep during a show and fall in front of thousands of fans."

"Shit, Sammy, I never thought of that." I scrape my hand down my face, like I need something new to worry about regarding Callum.

"I've tried to talk to him. When I do, he just tells me to fuck off. I can't help him if I don't know what the fuck the problem is in the first place." I sigh. "He mentioned that he was tired of always being the responsible one. But that's always been his role. So I think it's more. I dunno, man. I'm at a loss."

"How 'bout this? You go try to fix things with your girl. I'll try to get Cal to talk to me. He usually goes to you, but for some reason, he feels he can't. It can't hurt for me to give it a shot." He shrugs and hands me a bottle of water.

I down the water before standing. "Thanks, man. Text me if you can get him to talk."

Sam pats my back. "You know I will. Good luck, man. I think you're going to need it

R

TRYING TO LISTEN FOR MOVEMENT, I stand outside my hotel room. Our room. I'm trying to figure out if Becka is in there. If she is, is she asleep? How angry is she at me? She should be fairly pissed off. I would be if someone treated me the way I treated her last night. Does she have one foot out the door like Sammy thinks she might?

I let out a sigh and rest my forehead on the cool door for a minute before I slip my keycard out of my pocket and let myself in.

The first thing I see is the outfit she wore last night thrown on the little bench between the dresser and the closet, her heels tucked under the bench. Well, at least she hasn't packed herself up and left. She loves those heels, and she'd never leave without them.

Walking into our room, it's obvious she's not here. Her stuff is here, most of it scattered around the room, except for what she packed last night when she made a show like she was going to go sleep in Sammy's room if I didn't.

I grab the small trash can next to the desk and gingerly pick up the shards of glass from the tumbler I threw last night. I was trying to scare her. What a dick. Sammy's right. I need to grovel when she comes back. But where is she? I look for a note, but the little hotel notepad is glaringly blank, and my nearly dead phone has no unread messages.

I take a quick shower, and she's still not back when I'm out. I don't want to text her, asking where she's at, but I'm starting to get worried. Just as I grab my phone from where I left it charging, the door behind me swings open.

I turn and her eyes meet mine.

"Here you are!" I say it at the same time she says, "Oh. You're back." Her tone isn't one of excitement like mine is. But it isn't one of dread. It's just dead, with no emotion at all. Shit, this isn't good.

She's dressed in a pink and green workout outfit, clutching her magazine to her chest. I should have known. She likes to work out in the mornings. If we're in a hotel, she'll use the elliptical or treadmill in the fitness room. If we're just parked in the area, she'll go for a run around the inside of the stadium.

She glances away from my gaze and down toward the bed, then up at the artwork that is over the bed, at the TV, even though it's off, at the place where the whiskey stain is on the carpet where I just cleaned up the shattered glass. Then she looks over my shoulder, outside. She looks everywhere but at me.

I take a step toward her, but she takes a step back, so I stop my advance. I don't want her to think I'm trying to threaten her.

"I'd try groveling." Sam's voice is strong in my head. I don't even know how to grovel.

I put my hands up.

"Look, I said a lot of shit I didn't mean last night. I'm sorry, Becks. I was in a bad mood yesterday after some shit that went down during our media sessions, and I let that come between us. I'm sorry." I look up through my lashes at her. Girls always love when I do that.

"Okay." It's all she says. And she's still not looking at me.

Fuck, this isn't going my way. Maybe Sammy's right and she's got one foot out the door.

"I mean it, Becka. I'm really sorry I was a dick last night. I was obviously drunk, but that's not an excuse. It's just a fact. I can be an asshole when I'm drunk. I promise I don't get drunk that much anymore." I reach a hand out to her, hoping she'll take it.

"Good to know." She squeezes between me and the dresser, making sure she doesn't touch me. My heart sinks to my stomach when she doesn't even look at me, just puts her magazine down and kicks off her tennis shoes.

Becka grabs some clothes out of her bag. "I'm going to shower. Alone."

I nod, looking down at my shoes. I hope Sammy's having better luck with Callum than I am with Becka.

Chapter 24

Becka

After making sure to lock the bathroom door behind me, I turn on the shower to let it heat up before I get in. Mav's got another thing coming if he thinks he can be downright rude and hurtful. I don't deserve to be treated like that.

His mea culpa act isn't winning him any points. He can't just bat those frustratingly beautiful eyelashes of his and think that makes everything better. If anything, it pisses me off even more. Why do guys have beautiful thick lashes and us women have to use mascara and shit to make them look half as good as theirs? Ugh, just another infuriating man thing.

Kase said I needed to give him a chance to apologize. She hinted that this is probably just a misunderstanding. Our first real fight, I guess, but it's not something I want to celebrate. I didn't sleep well, wondering if Mav was sleeping okay, or if he was worried about me. But that's stupid. Sammy pretty much said he passed out after he got to his room. I hope he has the worst fucking hangover ever. He deserves it. I should have gone to Callum's after he left.

I finish up in the shower and take my time in the bathroom.

Once I lotion myself up from head to toe, I get dressed, putting on my makeup leisurely. I don't know what he has planned for today before the show tonight and, honestly, I don't really care.

When I come out, he's sitting on the couch, his head hung in his hands. He doesn't look up at me. It's then I realize how rough he looks. His hair is damp, so he's showered, but he has left it to air dry, which is not normal for him. He's a bit paler than usual, and generally looks like he doesn't feel good. Dammit, I wished a terrible hangover on him, and it came true. I'm trying to stay angry at him, but he looks so miserable.

I grab my magazine and lie down on the bed and pretend to read, but I can't. I'm thinking more about miserable Mav.

"I'm sorry." This time, his apology is a hoarse whisper. "If you want to leave, go home, I understand. I'll buy you the ticket." He glances at me from the side of his eye.

"Do you need a Tylenol or something?" I grab my purse and start to go through it, looking for the little Tylenol cylinder. I let two spill into my hand and grab him a water from the minibar.

He looks at my extended hand with the pills, and then up at me. "Go on. You look like you feel like shit."

He tentatively takes the pills and pops them into his mouth, and then downs the bottle of water.

"Uh, thanks." His voice is still raspy and rough.

"You're welcome." There's an uncomfortable weight in the room between us now that he's apologized. Like he's not sure where he stands with me.

"So, uh, Cal was really fucked up last night?" He looks gutted at the thought of his friend.

I nod slowly. "He seemed fine on the way to the club. Sammy and I were dancing, and when we went back to VIP, he had disappeared. We had our drinks, and then went back dancing, and midway through, he spotted Cal halfway up the light scaffolding. He had me get Jax while he went toward Cal."

Mav grimaces at the idea of Cal up there on the scaffolding.

"I don't understand why he won't talk to me about this dark cloud he has over him. The cocaine isn't the problem, but for some reason, he thinks it's the answer."

"What are you guys going to do?" I sit next to him and take his hand, intertwining our fingers, so he knows that I'm still here and I do still love him, even if I didn't like his behavior last night.

"He won't talk to me. Sammy's trying to talk to him right now."

As if on cue, there is a commotion in the hall, shouting and carrying on. And I swear one of the voices sounds like Sammy's. Mav jumps up and crosses the room in three steps, flinging the door open.

"He's in here. Hurry." Sammy's loud and insistent.

"Fuck." Mav takes off toward the commotion, and I follow.

A paramedic crew is coming down the hall toward us. Sammy pops his head out of Callum's room. "In here! He's in here!"

We follow the paramedics into the room to a chaotic scene with Callum, passed out cold with blue lips, on the floor in the middle of the room.

When Sammy sees Mav, it's like whatever was holding him together comes undone. "I was too late. I was too late again." Tears start streaming down his face as he looks up to Mav.

Mav grabs Sammy and pulls him in for a hug. "They'll help him. They gotta help him." They're both pale, and the concern etched into their foreheads ages them.

Paramedics rip Callum's shirt off and put those little pads on his chest. Another one puts an oxygen mask over his face, then gets an IV started.

"I can't... I can't. I just can't do this again. I don't know where Killian is. But I can't do this again, Mav. I'm sorry. I can't." Sammy shakes his head and pushes past him and out the door. I don't know if I should stay here, or if I should go after Sammy.

He's so distraught. Mav nods his head at me, as if he knows what I'm thinking, and then looks out the door Sammy just vacated.

I see him slip into his own room, so I follow him in.

"Hey, Sam." He jumps when I speak.

"Fuck, Becka. You scared the shit out of me. I'm sorry. You probably think I'm a pussy. But I just can't. Not after Seven. I can't watch that again." His bottom lip trembles. I don't know who Seven is, but I have a feeling it was his sister that Mav told me about.

I go to his minibar and get him some water, much like I did with Mav just minutes ago. "You should sit, Sammy."

I want to tell him it's going to be okay. I really do, but I don't dare. Because I've never seen someone with lips as blue as Callum's.

Since I can't reassure him with words, I sit next to him and pat his leg. He takes my hand and holds it, squeezing it tight. I'm the only reason he's hanging on right now, so I don't care what Mav or Cal or anyone else thinks. I'm going to comfort Sammy. I hope Cal doesn't die. We have crazy chemistry. Our sex is leaps and bounds better than what I have with Mavrick but maybe that's because it's taboo because of Mav. He's always pulling me off into closets and storage rooms at different arenas or hotels.

I don't wish death on anyone. But at least if Cal does OD, I'll still have Mav and I'll still be heading to Los Angeles at the end of the tour.

"What the fuck is... Cal!" The voice of a terrified man-boy rings out from the elevator bay near the center of the floor. It's not the deep voice of the brooding bassist. It's the broken voice of a terrified teenager.

Sammy and I look at each other and speak at the same time. "Killian!"

We stand up and head down the hall to try to catch him

before he stumbles into the scene of his twin brother half dead on the floor of his hotel. But we are too late.

But thank God, Killian doesn't walk in on what we did. Because Cal's now on a gurney, and semi-conscious.

"We're taking him to Memorial Hospital," the paramedic announces to us as they start wheeling Callum out of his room and toward the elevators. "He's stabilized for now."

When they push Cal past a terrified Killian, he shakes a finger as he's rolled past his twin brother and says, "Don't do drugs." Killian follows and goes into the ambulance with his brother.

We pile into a rideshare to the hospital, me sitting between Mav and Sam, each holding one of my hands, both squeezing tightly. I am where I am supposed to be. Once at the hospital, though, the only one they'll let back with Callum is his brother. We sit in the waiting room until others trickle in, our numbers doubled as we are joined by Jax, Darren from the record company, and Jeff, their road manager.

I hope Callum's okay. We aren't really getting updates. Mav and Sammy are both dealing with it differently. It's hard trying to be the calming factor, when I just really want to know how Callum is too.

After what seems like hours, Killian comes out. His face is drawn in and serious as he comes and stands in front of us.

"So, um, he's doing okay. He's kind of groggy and shit. They think he got some coke laced with an anesthetic. The doctor said it's all the rage right now. Anyway, his heart and brain both look fine. They're saying we were lucky today. And we should be thankful to you, Sam, for calling it in, because it could have gone south really quickly if someone hadn't found them when they did."

Sammy releases a breath that it seems like he's been holding since we got here. "He's going to be okay?" he asks. Kill nods. "Oh, thank God." Sammy grips his knees and buries his head and hands, letting out a noise that is part relief and part terror.

Killian hugs Sammy. "Thank you for calling the ambulance, man. Thank you for checking on him."

He looks up at Mav. "Um, you guys want to see him? I can take you both back for a few minutes. Sorry, Becka."

"No worries. Go." I urge both Mav and Sam. This isn't the time to be worried about me. They should be with Callum. He needs them.

Chapter 25

Callum

Fuck me, that was close.

I think I almost died. Or maybe I did, and they brought me back. I'm not sure what just happened.

But fuck, that was close. I need to straighten my shit. I don't want to end up next to Sevenya.

Sevenya. I saw her while I was in my fucked-up, half-dead state. She kept saying something that didn't make sense to me. It still doesn't. "Take care of him. He's going to need it when he finds out what I did.

Obviously, my mind was fucked because she should know we'd take care of Sammy.

Chapter 26

Mavrick

Callum's acting ornery with the nurse, giving her a hard time, but that's all it is, an act. He feels better, and what's more, he looks two hundred percent better than he did just hours ago. So does Sammy. Callum probably doesn't even realize he took about eight years off Sammy's life today with the little stunt he pulled. I can't help the sigh that escapes me, and when it does, Callum glances my way.

The doctor left about five minutes ago, telling us we need to let him rest, but someone can stay the night with him. That will be Killian, of course, and there won't be an argument from me or Sam about it.

"I guess Mav and I should hit it." Sammy stands from sitting on the side of Callum's bed. "You heard the doc. Rest is the best medicine."

"Actually," I say, standing up straight from the wall I was leaning against. "Can you guys give me and Cal a few minutes?"

I'm worried Killian will flip out on me, but he nods and moves toward the door behind Sam.

"Come on, Kill, I know where the cafeteria is. Let's get

something to eat. I'm sure you're hungry. I sure the fuck am."
They head down the hall to the bank of elevators.

When I turn to Cal's bed, he sits up a little bit and fusses with the sheet around his legs.

I take Sammy's place and lean against the foot of Cal's bed. My heart is both happy as fuck that I can sit here and talk to him, and heavy as hell, because he's in this position in the first place.

"Look, Mav," he starts, but I interrupt him.

"I'm not here to try to get you to talk to me or any of that shit. Been there, done that, gave up on the book coming out." He blinks at me, his face still. "I've let you know many times that I'm worried about you, man. And it's because of this. Right here. At least we were lucky this time."

"There won't be a next time." His voice is solemn, but I don't know if I can believe it.

"Whatever. You've said that before too. Yet somehow here we are. I told you; you were either going to kill yourself jumping off something or overdose. Cal, don't make me be right."

I pause, trying to decide how to word what I want to say to him. I don't want to push him, because I still think that there is something going on with him. Then I decide, fuck it, I'm giving him the brutal truth.

"You aged Sammy about eight years today when he walked in on you. Thank fuck, he had enough wherewithal to call 911. And thank fuck for Becka, too, because she sat with him while the fucking paramedics revived your ass. He couldn't be in the same room. Because he looked at you, half-dead and blue, and saw his dead fucking sister, Callum. I did too. That's on you. All on you... Fuck!" I stand up with a kick to his bed. I'm being hard on him. But he has to see that his actions have fucking consequences.

"You are on this self-destructive path, and I've been telling you it's going to kill you, and today... well, today, it almost did."

"Mav, I—"

"No, Callum. No excuses. Fix your shit. Deal with your shit. Whatever that shit is. Because I got a lovely glimpse as to what that day is going to be like. I'm going to have to deal with both Sammy and Kill losing their respective shits, and I'm only one person...and when do I get to lose my shit because my best friend destroyed himself? When he knew better." I stop. I might be a selfish sonofabitch, but I don't want to lose him to his stupidness and have to deal with their grief too.

"Anyway," I say as I stand, hearing Sammy and Killian returning from their little foraging adventure. "It's time to grow a pair and grow up, brother. And that's all I'm going to say." I walk right out of the room without looking back.

Chapter 27

Becka

Despite the show being cancelled for the night, everyone is exhausted after Callum's near-death experience. Sammy, Mav, and me ride share back to the hotel, leaving Kill with Cal at the hospital. The doctor was pretty sure he'll be discharged late tomorrow. "You wanna hang with us for a bit? We can all get some room service and watch a movie and just chill?" Mav asks Sammy as we get into the elevator at the hotel.

Sammy shakes his head solemnly. Even when visiting with Cal, Sammy's demeanor has been serious. He's not the normal, lighthearted Sammy that everyone loves.

"I'm good. I'm just gonna hit the hay, I think." He gets in and pushes the button for our floor.

"You sure you're good, man?" There's something in Sammy's demeanor that's causing Mav's lips pull down into a slight frown, even though Sammy nods.

"Just tired." We split ways when we get out of the elevator.

"Hey, Sam?" Mav calls to the drummer, who turns around and looks at him. "You need anything, you text or call me. Promise." Mav holds his phone up.

"I will." Sam turns and Mav stays to watch him go into his room, before heaving a sigh and picking my hand back up.

We walk wordlessly back into our room.

Mav looks at me with a wry grin. "Um, now, what were we talking about?"

"It seems like a week ago when we were last in this room." I don't even remember putting my shoes back on after my shower. But I must have at some point because I'm wearing them.

He nods and pulls me to him. "I really am sorry. I know I said it before, but I was a dick. I'll try to do better." He kisses the tip of my nose, then drops down to reward me with a tender kiss on the lips.

"If you want or need to go home, you can. I know I messed up big time."

I grab him tight and press myself into his body. He wraps his arms around me and pulls me to him. I don't want to go home. I want to stay right here. Even if things don't work out with Mav, which I'm sure they will, I'm staying on this tour.

I rest my head on his chest and listen to his heart. He kisses the top of my head, and then pulls me toward the bed and hands me the remote.

"Pick something to watch. What do you want from room service? I'm sure you're as hungry as I am."

"I could eat." I scan through the options on the schedule. "I'll have the chicken tacos." He nods and calls down for room service while kicking off his boots, and I flip through the movie guide on the TV. I don't really care what we watch, so I pick something action-oriented for Mav.

Pulling off his pants, he joins me on the bed. "They said it'll be 20 minutes. Well, originally, they said 45 minutes to an hour. I told them that there'd be a hundred buck tip in it if they could get it to me in under 30."

He curls his lips on one side. "Sometimes it's good to be a

rock star." He lounges next to me on the bed, but damn, he looks exhausted. I snuggle with him, and he pulls me to him.

"Becks? Are we okay?" he rasps quietly.

I nod and snuggle into him harder. He drops off within minutes. I stay still against him, so that he gets as much sleep as possible before our food comes.

There's a quiet knock on the door, and I get up and grab the tip he left on the dresser. I indicate for the waiter to be quiet as he rolls the tray with our food in. Slipping him the hundred bucks, he quietly exits our room a happy guy.

Despite my efforts to remain quiet, when I turn back to the bed, my sleeping prince is awake. His head is resting on his hand, his elbow supporting them. He still looks tired, but he has that dopey love-sick smile that he used to get when we first met. A smile that's been missing from his face.

"Sorry, I was trying to be quiet. You looked so peaceful sleeping."

"No worries, my nose woke me up. I'm hungry." He sits up when I push the cart closer to the bed.

We sit side by side, cross-legged with our knees touching while we eat from the tray.

He devours his cheeseburger so fast that I end up offering him my third taco, which he gratefully eats as well.

"Told you I was hungry. Are you sure you got enough?" I nod, and he gets up and pushes the room service cart out into the hall.

When he returns, he crosses his hands across his bare chest and looks down on me. "I am sorry for the way I acted, Becks."

"I know, you've been saying that a lot. Yes, you hurt me. But we're good now." I reach my arms out and he walks into them. I hug him tight, my head resting on his abdomen. I look up at him just as his phone rings out with a text. Grabbing it, he reads the message and looks up at me.

"Sammy is wondering if it's okay if he comes to watch a

movie with us after all." His lips pull down. I know he's asking me, but I know damn well if I don't say yes, he'll look at me differently. Still, I'd rather be alone, just me and Mav.

Sammy was okay at the hospital after we knew Callum was going to recover, and it helped that when Killian brought us back to his room, Callum was with it. I still wonder if he waited as long as he did for Sammy's benefit more than anything.

"Of course. Should I get room service to send up a variety of snacks since our minibar is pretty dry?"

He nods. "Good idea. He's always hungry anyway."

Mav moves the chair in our room, so it faces the TV. "Hey, look, this chair's a pull-out bed." He pulls it out.

"That explains the extra bedding on the shelf in the closet."

"There is?" Mav turns towards me.

"Toss it over." I yank it down from the shelf and Mav pulls the chair out and makes it up for Sammy. "Just in case he stays long enough to fall asleep."

"Good idea. I bet he's wrecked, and I doubt he got in a nap like we did."

Mav nods as he tucks the fitted sheet around the chair. "True. Although it wasn't that long of a nap."

"I know, but you obviously needed it."

I watch as he expertly makes up the pull-out chair, then comes around the bed to me and pulls me to him tight in a hug. "Thank you for being cool about Sammy coming over. For letting me nap. For taking care of Sammy when he needed someone. And most of all, for forgiving me."

"Of course," I murmur into his neck. Mav always smells so good. It's his cologne but also him.

Soon, there is a knock on the door, and Mav lets in Sammy an exhausted looking Sammy with has a bag of chips in his hand.

"Look what we discovered. Our chair turns into a pull-out.

You can just relax here with us and be comfy in case you fall asleep." Mav pats the pull-out.

"Cool. Thanks." His feet are bare and he's wearing black basketball shorts and a tank top, which I figure is the Sammy equivalent to pajamas, since he wears a similar ensemble in the mornings on the bus.

I think all of the guys have upped their modesty since I've been around. I figure they probably all walked around in their skivvies before me, not really caring. That would be fun to see. Sometimes I wonder what it would be like to be on the bus when they think it's just them.

Mav hands him the remote as room service knocks on the door again. "You pick," he tells Sam as he heads to the door and lets the waiter in with the huge tray of appetizers. Way more than three people would normally eat, but I've seen Sammy eat firsthand. When he's hungry, he can pack the food away.

Sam makes himself a plate, taking a little bit of everything and sits up on the folded-out bed.

Mav starts the movie that Sammy chose. The first Fast & Furious, which is kind of a surprise, seeing as the movie is kind of old. He just shrugs when the movie starts.

After we watch the first movie, Sammy starts the second, but it's not soon into it that Mav nudges me, and then nods to Sam, who is sound asleep. Mav leans over that side of the bed and covers Sam with the extra blanket, and then we get in our bed and snuggle up together, him spooning me. He kisses the crown of my head and whispers, "You rock."

Chapter 28

Mavrick

We stay in the hotel for an extra night. Darren sent the crew and buses ahead to the next stop, and we'll fly in on the day of the show. This gives Callum an extra day to gain his equilibrium back after nearly overdosing. He seems okay. He claims he just feels a little tired. The doctor highly suggested that Cal get himself in a recovery program of some sort. I know the stubborn sonofabitch won't, though.

When we finally hit the road again, Callum seems to be keeping on the straight and narrow. He'll have the occasional beer when we're all hanging out together, but I haven't even seen him so much as smoke a blunt since that night three weeks ago.

When we start the third leg of this tour, our East Coast leg, we seem to be gelling like the band we used to be. One good thing about Callum's near-death experience is that Killian sure as fuck has straightened up. He doesn't even drink now, for the most part. Nothing hard, anyway. Rarely even a beer. Mostly, he sticks to water, with the occasional soda.

Becka, on the other hand, is starting to annoy the fuck out

of me. She not only seems to be drinking more than she had been on the last leg of the tour, but she seems to be clingier as well. I'm pretty sure it's just life on the road, because usually by the end of the tour, the band can't stand to look at each other. We'll all go our separate ways for a week or two, but then we are right as rain and ready to write.

> Me: I'm doing a rock podcast. I'm not going to be there for at least another hour or so.

> Becka: Mav! You promised. I'm bored and I wanted some time to hang out before the show.

> Me: Sorry Becks. Work calls.

Her silence is deafening. She's pissed off. But we are trying to engage all media types, and this podcast is one that I actually like listening to. Being invited to be a guest is cool as fuck. No way am I passing up this opportunity.

It's probably more like an hour and a half, because I stay a little after the show to chat with the hosts, John and Andrew, about the state of the music industry and how it's changed with streaming. They are cool guys, and I make sure that Darren sets them up with backstage access for the show tonight and that they know they are more than welcome in the green room.

> Cal: Just saw your girl. She isn't pleased with you right now.

> Me: No way am I passing up a chance to be on The Rock Show with John and Drew! They are really cool dudes.

> Cal: Just warning you. She seems sensitive lately.

> Me: Thanks for the heads up man.

When I get back to the hotel, Becka is at the pool, drinking something with an umbrella. I watch from afar as she makes sure the pool attendant sees her scantily covered tits. He is polite to her, but obviously not interested. I'm sure he's seen it all in his line of work. She then attempts to flirt with Sammy, by practically shoving her boobs in his face. I can't tell if he's not interested, or he truly doesn't get what she's seemingly offering up to whomever will take it.

The sting of a man-slap on my back has me turning my head quickly in time to see Dom standing next to me, also surveying the pool area. He's lucky I didn't deck him. When I'm startled like that, I tend to come back fighting as a reflex.

"Your girl's acting kind of needy, Mav. You not keeping her satisfied in bed?" He chuckles at me. "I've had her. She's not that great."

I pull my hand back and am about to let it fly when someone grabs my arm, preventing me from striking. Callum's voice is in my ear. "You know Dom's stirring shit on purpose. Let it go. If you hit him, it'll end up in a huge fight and a PR disaster for Darren. Not to mention, all over the internet." He nods to the paparazzi standing on the other side of the pool fence. "He'll get his in the end. Karma always comes for people like him."

I relax. Callum's got my back. He knows what a dick Dom can be. I nod and walk away, toward my fiancée.

"Finally. I was so bored." She pouts like a fucking teenage girl, something she only does when she's been drinking. "I thought you were my fiancée. Aren't you supposed to do stuff with me?"

"I'm here. We can do whatever you want for the next two and a half hours, Becks."

She sighs and flops back against the pool chair. "I wanted to spend the whole day with you. Not just another wham-bam-thank-you-ma'am and off you go." She purses her lips together and looks at me, tipping her chin up in the air slightly.

"Look, Becks. This is my job. It pays for all your clothes and shopping trips and stuff. Sometimes, I have to work." I feel kind of dickish pointing this out to her, but this is my career. I love music, and I will work as hard as I can to do this for the rest of my damn life, or as close to it as I can get anyway.

"Hmph." She folds her arms across those tits of hers and, suddenly, I am angry at her. She's been shoving those tits in everyone's faces because I wasn't here, and now she's got them covered. I don't understand her.

"I'm sorry you're upset. I'm going up to the room if you want to join me. Or stay at the pool, if you'd rather." I turn on my heel and head upstairs. It'll be interesting to see if she follows me.

This same scene plays out week after week, show after show, and it's starting to get old. I love her, but I don't love her attitude lately. Not to mention that I think Cal's using again. He seemed off during tonight's show. He'd been so strait-laced until tonight. I can't wait until we play the last show of this leg of the tour. It's the one I've been most looking forward to, because it's at the one venue I've always wanted to play. Madison Square Garden.

Then Becks and I can go home and figure out when we want to get married. Get into a real routine. Maybe we can have her friend come out to visit us. I know she misses Kasey.

"Did you happen to see Callum before the show tonight?" I ask Becks when we get back to our hotel room. We are playing three shows here in Florida and have this room for four days. It's nice when we can be rooted in one place for a few days. Especially at this point in the tour, because all that togetherness on the bus is a whole lot.

"Why? It's not like we hang out," she says and her head snaps to me.

"I was just wondering because he seemed off today onstage. I thought maybe he might be on something again and wondered if you saw him is all."

She shakes her head. "I just saw him around the hotel here and there. I took a ride share to the mall to walk around and ended up eating there. When I came back, he was by the elevators like he was going back up to his room from being out. But like I said, it's not like we hang out, so I'm not sure where he'd been. He didn't even hold the elevator car for me. I had to wait for the next one. But maybe he didn't see me."

Maybe. Or maybe, he was high as a fucking kite and didn't want her to see him. At least he hasn't tried to jump off anything yet. I sigh. Callum, my brother, what the fuck is going on with you?

"Enough about Callum. Let's make the most of the time we have before the show." She starts stripping and encouraging me to do the same.

She's already ready for me.

"Let me get a rubber." I turn from her to my suitcase to grab one.

"Is that even necessary? We are engaged to be married." She huffs her bangs at me. It is such a turn-off when she acts like a fucking teenager.

"Yes. I told you. No love without a glove. I don't want kids. Not because I wasn't married or in a relationship. Because I don't want kids. Non-negotiable."

"What if I do?"

"Then we need to talk. Because I don't. Not now. Not later. Kids are a dealbreaker for me, Becks. Is that going to be a problem? Because if so, we should probably consider parting ways." I'm pretty sure I was upfront with her about not wanting kids. This shouldn't be news to her.

"I thought it was because you didn't know me then. You didn't want kids with just anybody."

I can't shake my head fast enough. "I don't want kids. Period. It's a dealbreaker for me." I pull on my sweatpants. This isn't going to happen until we get this straightened out. If we get it straightened out. "You need to think long and hard if you are okay with being with someone who doesn't want kids."

She pulls on a t-shirt and sits cross-legged on the bed. "Are you sure you'll never want to have kids?"

She looks up at me from where she sits cross-legged on the bed. I nod. "I'm pretty darn sure. I didn't have a great child-hood. Hell, none of the Rebels have. Not only do I think I'm not fatherhood material, but I have my career to think about. I don't know that I could do what I love and be a father."

"I could help. I'd take care of the baby and anything it needed."

I shake my head slowly. "Plus, what if we don't work out for the long run, but have this kid. What if you get tired of me, or decide you hate the rock life and we split? How is that fair to the kid? I am just not interested in a future that involves a child, Becks. I've been nothing but on the up and up about this since day one."

I think this is it. My throat clenches. I do love her, but not enough to go back on one of my most sacred vows to myself. If I do that, then what kind of man am I? Not one of his word, and if you can't keep your word to yourself, can you keep it with other people?

She's quiet for a long time. I finally sit on the chair in our room while she considers it.

"I'm okay with it," she says finally. Her voice is quiet.

"Are you sure? Because I don't want to take something from you that you really want." She nods before I'm even done asking the question.

"I'm sure, Mav. Really. It's probably for the best. I mean, I didn't have the best parents in the world either." She shrugs. "I love you and I know that you love me. And that is all that matters to me."

She gets up from the bed and comes and sits on my lap, kissing and snuggling up with me.

"You're absolutely sure?"

"Absolutely." I can feel her resolve in the way she kisses me.

"I can't wait for the Garden. And then to take you home and settle in. We can start talking about the when and where of our wedding."

"I've already bought a couple of bridal magazines and marked things I like and don't like. Do you want to see?" She smiles up at me.

"Sure."

She goes to her suitcase and pulls out some magazines, complete with those little tag thingies on pages she's marked, and returns to my lap. We spend the rest of the time before we head out to the arena going through them, and she adds some of the things I mention to her to notes she's already made.

Chapter 29

Becka

Just a couple more weeks and this tour will be over. I am ready to get to Los Angeles with Mav. He's promised when we get home, he'll arrange for a credit card for stuff for the wedding so I can start planning right away. He's even promised me that I can invite Kasey over to help with the rest of the wedding planning.

Mav's so excited to play Madison Square Garden. I guess it's one of the places he's always wanted to play, but they just never had it on their tour before. He's also excited because Diminished Capacity is going first, so the Blind Rebels get to close out the night. I've purchased a special outfit, with an even more special outfit underneath. Just for Mav.

I know that Killian, Sammy, and Mav are still worried about Callum. He's not really been using anything too hard, I don't think, but he's been drinking a lot more again. At first, after his OD, he was straight and barely drank at all and did no drugs, not even pot. But now the beer has given way to hard liquor, and I didn't want to mention it to Mav, but I did see him smoking pot with some guys from the crew.

It wouldn't surprise me if, after the tour, they make him go to rehab or AA or something like that.

He's stopped doing crazy things like trying to launch himself off balconies, but Mav still insists that this is not the way Callum usually behaves. I probably don't know him enough, but he's not, um, lacking by any means.

He seems like a typical rocker to me. Reckless and a little bit wild, maybe on the edge of out of control. I mean, isn't that the appeal of a rock star anyway? They are the people who do the stuff that regular men only think or dream of doing. That is why they are rock stars and other people are... well, plain, ordinary people.

Mav is not as crazy as Callum, but he's most definitely not plain or ordinary, which is why I love that he's mine. Even though he's not as attentive as he used to be.

That's because this is the last big push of this tour. These are places the guys haven't been in a while, or sometimes ever. The market needs to see and hear them on the radio, on the TV, on the internet, in most of these local areas. If it was up to me, I'd be sitting on his lap for every interview. The media takes most of his time away from me, and I do not love that at all.

That's what sucks about the media part. It's mostly Mav they want to talk to. Sometimes it's the whole band, or Mav and Callum. But mostly, it's just Mav. That's what happens when you're the lead singer. You're the entire focal point of the band. Plus, with Callum being so on edge lately, I think Darren is worried something weird will come out of his mouth that will end in a whole PR disaster, so most of the time, Cal's excluded, and that's fine by me.

When I am bored and Callum is around, I seek him out. I'm trying to "help" him. For Mav. Like Cal, I know what it's like to be left behind, to see your friends in relationships and not having any time for you anymore. Plus, Cal gives me a little something Mav doesn't seem to have time for lately. Attention.

Also, when he's hanging out with me, that means he's not hanging out with Dominick. Dom is bad news. I'm pretty sure he has it in for me. It bugs him that he threw away his chance with me, and Mav has my heart.

I think Dom is trying to plant seeds of hate for me in Callum's head in the hopes that Cal and I won't get along, which will break me and Mav up. But if it were to come to that, I am pretty sure Mav would walk away from the Rebels for me. He loves me that much. I mean, I have the ring to prove it. And there is no way I'd run to Dom like he thinks I would.

By keeping Cal away from Dom, I'm only worried about Mav finding out about our dalliances.

"Hey, Cal. Whatcha up to?" I ask on my way back up to the room from the pool. It's the only time I get out unless I take a rideshare somewhere. And I try not to do that too much, even though Mav is paying for them.

He shrugs one shoulder. "Nothin' special. Why?" We wait at the elevator bank together. They almost always have us all on the same floor, which is nice. Except when it's awkward because I'm worried Sammy or Killian will see me leaving Cal's room and sneaking back over to Mav's room.

But it seems that Callum's grown something of a conscience lately. I don't think he realizes that I know the first couple of times he was testing my loyalty to Mav. Until I got under his skin, that is.

"Just trying to be friendly. I don't have an ulterior motive, Cal." I raise up my hands. "Look. I get bored. I miss Mav. I just wanted some human interaction that wasn't with hotel staff, and Sammy's off somewhere with Killian, getting tattoos. Sorry I bothered you."

I flip open my magazine as we get into the elevator and basically tune him out on the ride up to our room. Our elevator finally dings, and I look up and step forward to get out of the elevator, when Cal touches my elbow.

"Hey. I'm sorry."

I shrug away from him slightly, putting a step between us. "Okay."

"Look, I feel bad for being rude. Do you want to go have lunch somewhere?"

"Really? You want to have lunch with me?" He usually doesn't want to be seen out together.

"I mean, sure, why not? I'm hungry. Are you?"

"Well, yeah. I am." But I am also dressed in a bright yellow bikini right now.

He nods. "Okay. Go change and meet me by the elevators in thirty minutes?"

Chapter 30

Mavrick

I finally see the light that is the end of the tunnel that is this hellacious tour. Things seem to be going well right now, but I don't want to jinx it. Callum is now getting drunk off his ass more than he used to, but at least his recent death wish seems to have abated. For now, anyway. Best I can tell, he's not using drugs of any sort, even though the drinking is way too much.

After this tour, we are having a heart-to-heart, and he might not like the results. But I'm trying really hard not to think about that.

In just a few days, my ultimate rock star dream will come true, playing Madison Square Garden. Plus, we have a few days off right now, and it's with limited media. I can't wait to surprise Becka with that news. I have one media engagement early this morning, and then I am hers until 8:00 p.m. tomorrow when we play the Saratoga Performing Arts Center. Then the next day, it's the Garden.

We arrived in New York early this morning, checked in, and crashed. She's still asleep and looks so beautiful and peaceful.

Her wavy blonde hair surrounds her head and gives her an almost angelic look. But she's anything but angelic in bed.

I know this leg of our tour has been hard on her. Pretty much the last three months, we've been going at it hard, with few off days between shows and lots of media on the off days.

I tried to spend as much time as I could with her, but I know she's been lonely. We've really been pushing hard with the media in this market because it's not one of our better ones. We haven't been on the East Coast in a bit. So we dogged the media... and by media, I mean all media. Traditional, social, print. All of it.

But it was to the detriment of Becks, I'm sure. I hope to make up for it with some time devoted to just her today and tomorrow.

Maybe when we get home, I should buy her dog. She could bring it on the next tour. Kind of my consolation prize for not wanting kids. I could have a dog. She might like it. That's it. When we get back to Malibu, I'm buying her a dog. Something small she can carry around. But not one of those nervous Yorkie things. I am sure we can find something that will work for her.

I lean in and kiss her temple lightly. "Becks?"

She groans lightly and swats at me. "Too early. Put that thing away."

I can't help but chuckle at her. "My thing is away. I have media."

"What's new?" She rolls over, her back to me, and snuggles into her pillow, pulling the sheet tight around her shoulders.

"I'll be back before breakfast, I promise. Be dressed. We have reservations for brunch at this place downtown that the concierge suggested. Food's supposed to be amazing. Our reservation is at 10:00. Love you, Becks." Leaving a gentle kiss behind her ear, I get up and head out the door.

It's nine by the time I get back from doing the podcast recording. I've brought her a coffee. I hope I got it right, but let's be honest, I have no idea how she drinks her coffee. I should know these things.

"Hey, Becks, you up yet?" I call out as I come in. "I brought you a coffee."

"Oh cool. Thanks." She sticks her hand out of the bathroom, and I place the coffee in her grip. "I was wondering if I dreamed what you said to me this morning." She hangs her head out of the bathroom, hair wet and face bare.

"What, that I love you?" I lean in and kiss her nose.

"No, you were taking me to breakfast." She leans back in and continues putting her makeup on.

"Nope. We have reservations and everything, Becks. The concierge made them because this place fills up quick this time of year. And I listened to him because I didn't want to have to pull the rock star card at the hostess stand to take you someplace nice. I planned!" My jokes hit right, and she rewards me with a little smile. Something that's been missing from her face lately. Probably because of my crazy schedule.

"Is your headache better?" I rub her shoulders as she stands in front of the mirror. She's been getting headaches a lot lately. I'm hoping they're from the stress of the tour. But if she is still having them when we get back to Malibu, we'll have to get her an appointment with someone.

"It's okay. Still there, but nothing like it was yesterday. Thanks for asking." She turns to face me and tips up to kiss me. I get lost in her as we kiss. It's my favorite place to be. Never in a million years would I have thought I'd have found my home in a woman I met on tour.

Luckily, she comes to her senses and pulls away. "Stop. I still have to dry my hair before we leave. We don't want to be late for brunch." She turns back to the mirror, picking up the hair dryer.

I order a car to meet us out front, and we walk hand-in-hand into the hip breakfast place, right on time for our reservations.

"This place is so cute," she raves as we are seated. They bring us both mimosas, and she sets hers down and asks for water too.

When we are alone, she looks at me with seriousness in those light blue eyes of hers. "What is this all about?"

"What do you mean, Becks?"

"This fancy brunch. Why?"

"Because I know I've been absent with all the media we've been doing. I didn't love being away from you. I haven't shown it the best, but I miss you too, you know." When I take her hand and hold it, she squeezes. "I love you. I have been kind of... I don't know, neglectful?" I sigh.

"You have." She nods her agreement. "But I know what you're doing. It's not like you are out there screwing other people, Mav. You are working, and I've tried to learn that this is your job, and it's important to you. It's been hard for me, but I get that this is your life. You're going to be my husband, so it's my life too." She sips her water, then sets it down.

"Thank you for that. For the understanding. But the good news is, not only are we nearly at the end of the tour, but I have the rest of today and up until the show at the Saratoga Performing Arts Center tomorrow to spend with you. And I plan to spend it with you, doing whatever you want to do. Anything. You want to shop, let's shop. You want to see a movie, I'll download the app and get us tickets right now. I mean it, Becks. This is our time together. Let's have fun."

Her eyes are watery. Crap. I hope she doesn't cry.

"You mean it?"

I nod, and she starts sniffling. "Thank you! That's awesome. Almost two full days with just us? I love you." She gets up and hugs me. "I don't know what's wrong with me. I'm happy! I promise," she says as she sits back in her chair across from me.

"I get it. I haven't been around. And when I am, I know I've been kind of, well, distracted by Cal's behavior. I promise, I'll try to do better, Becks." I sigh. "When we get back home, I'm going to have a sit-down with him and talk to him about this tour. About his drug and alcohol use. Ask him to get help. I'm worried about him. Sam's worried about him. And Killian's been his constant companion lately. I love Cal. He's my brother, and I'm worried about him. But I'm also going to work on myself and not let things come between you and me."

"You know what I'm looking forward to the most when we get back to Malibu?" Her eyes are sparkly now and less watery, which makes me feel better.

"Having Kase come visit?" She's been talking about Kasey a lot lately. She truly misses her friend.

Becka surprises me by shaking her head. "Getting my ring back from the jeweler." She flashes her hand up at me, a small cheap ring in its place. I needed something as a placeholder when we took her ring to be sized, but it's not even close to being the same. It's her "just until" ring.

"I'll make sure we can pick it up on the way home from the airport, even if I have to pay the guy to stay open just for us." My lips touch hers lightly.

Her face softens as she looks at me. "Really? You'd do that?"

"Absolutely. You're worth it."

I don't know if it's the excitement of nearly two days together or what, but Becks doesn't eat much of her omelet.

"Are you feeling okay?" I grab another piece of bacon and shove it into my mouth.

"I'm just so excited to spend time with you. I don't care what we do! Is there something that you want to do?"

"You mean besides you?" Her light blue eyes darken as she

about spits out the mouthful of orange juice she just took, and her lips curl up in the best way.

"I'm done." She pushes her plate away from her, just as a waiter happens to be walking by.

"I'll take that plate then." He grabs her plate and turns to take mine. "Are you done, sir?"

"I am. We have someplace to be."

Chapter 31

Becka

T hings are crazy backstage tonight. The Saratoga Performing Arts Center is an interesting place. The stage and part of the seats are covered, but the rest of the seats are on a huge, uncovered lawn area.

I walk around backstage. Sometimes, this is my favorite part. Just wandering around, taking in the parts of the show the fans don't see. Tonight, Diminished Capacity is playing last. Tomorrow night, at The Garden, as Mav calls it, the Rebels are the last to play, and Mav is tickled pink about how that worked out. He's not happy with co-headlining. He says they are way too popular for that crap and doesn't see this kind of tour happening in the future.

"Oh, hey, Becka." Giz waves me over. Technically, he's Killian's tech, but I'm friends with all the crew guys. And sometimes, Domino will tech for Killian, and then Giz will tech for Callum. I don't understand the whys of it. But I figure it's good to be friendly with all the crew guys. Mav's tech is Steven right now, but I don't think he'll be sticking around for the next tour. Mav's not that pleased with him for treating his acoustic poorly.

"I found some stools. Do you want me to set one up for you by the side of the stage for the show tonight?"

"That would be amazing! Thanks!" I high-five him, as that's a Giz thing. It's not just me who he high-fives, he high-fives everyone. Unless it's a kid, and then he low-fives them.

"If you're looking for Mav, I think I saw him go to catering." He waves and heads off in his own direction.

I was actually looking for Callum, but I probably should go find Mav first. He's been tuned to eleven all afternoon. He's so excited to get through this show so he can play at Madison Square Garden tomorrow. It's adorable.

I head away from the stage and toward the catering area. I need to grab a bottle of water anyway.

I'm almost to the catering area when I get grabbed under the arms and pulled backwards into the men's room. Startled, I start to scream when a hand goes over my mouth. I relax instantly. It's a hand I know intimately. One that's been all over my body. And the smell comforts me, so I relax into his arms.

"Thank God. Wanna guess how long I've been waiting for you? Let's just say, I was starting to feel like a perv hanging out in this bathroom."

"I've been looking for you too. We need to talk, Callum." He pulls me to him and kisses up my neck and behind my ear the spot that has me pressing my thighs together.

"Well, you've got me. But before we talk," he says as his hands push up my shirt, right under my bra, and squeeze, his nails digging into my skin, just how I like it.

This is so wrong of us. I think that's why it feels so good. I moan against his jaw. I can't help it.

I love Mav. But Callum's just so damn good. I find myself craving him lately, even when I'm with Mav. "Fuck, Cal."

"Exactly what I've been waiting for, babe." He pushes my skirt up over my hips, and the side of his face lifts in a half grin when he notices I'm commando today. He groans.

145

"God, you're always ready and willing, aren't you?" He undoes his pants and pushes them down just enough so I can grab his ass cheeks and pull him to me.

He walks us toward the cold, white-tiled wall and lifts my legs over his hips, entering me hard and fast. "Cal! Fuck yessss."

Unlike Mav, Cal is all sexy grunts and not much talking as the sounds of our bodies slapping against each other echo off the tile of the men's room.

Over his shoulder, I watch Callum piston into me in the bathroom mirror, loving how he plows into me hard, with desperate purpose. It's *me* making him wild like this, and that makes me powerful, which is even better than loved. I'm not delusional. Callum doesn't love me. He loves fucking me. But that will probably change when I tell him what I have to tell him.

He leans down, pulling my nipple into his mouth. Increasing his thrusts, he grazes my nipple with his teeth, running them back and forth over my sensitive flesh.

He knows it gets me off faster than anything, and this time is no exception as I come quickly on his next thrust. "Oh yes! Cal!" I dig my nails into his t-shirt clad arms as my entire body tenses, and then sparkles take over my field of vision.

He keeps pumping until he shouts out with his release. When he finishes pulsating within me, he walks us together as one unit to the bathroom counter, and gently sets me down before slipping out and cleaning up before tucking himself back into his jeans.

"Cal. We need to talk." I hold on to his forearms, their tattooed colors a contrast to my pale tone.

"Can it wait till tomorrow? We go on soon."

I shake my head. I am just going to have to tell him. Right here, right now, in the men's restroom, backstage in Saratoga.

"Cal, I'm pregnant."

He freezes and looks up at me, belt undone, eyes wide. I watch his Adam's apple move with his visible gulp. "Pregnant?"

He stares at me, stiff, holding the ends of his belt in his hands. "As in, having a baby? Fuck, Mav is not going to like that, Becks. He told you he didn't want kids. He's been that way since I've known him."

"Mav practically double wraps himself and dips it in spermicide every single time we do it. You and I... well..." I shrug. We've never worn condoms. Because I told him I'm on the pill. I'm not. I do take a pill every day when I remember, but it's not birth control.

He can only look at me, frozen in place, like a freaking statue. He grows pale, which makes his dark blue eyes look even darker.

"Callum. We are pregnant. You and me. I mean, I can tell Mav it's his, I guess. If that's what you want. But he's going to be surprised when it comes out with blue eyes."

Chapter 32

Callum

I'm completely fucked.

Chapter 33

Becka

The blood drains from Callum's face as his jaw slacks open.

"My baby? You're sure. Like 100% sure that you are pregnant and the baby is mine?"

I am so sure this baby is his. "Like I said, Mav wraps himself up like he's a damn germaphobe. You and I have never used protection."

"You said you were on the pill."

"I exaggerated." I smile coyly at him. "I take a pill every day. It's just not birth control."

"Should you be taking anything, knowing that you're pregnant?" His eyes widen with the realization that his baby is in me. "I mean, fuck, meds can fuck up a baby."

"Don't worry. I stopped taking them a little before I found out. I ran out. I'm sure it's fine. It was a super low dose anyway."

He swallows hard.

"I really think we should tell Mav about the baby, Cal. I mean, it's only right."

"Are you trying to destroy me, my band? Is that why you're here? Is that why you're with Mav?"

149

"No, Cal. I love Mav. What we did…well, that was a mistake, and now we have a baby. I can tell him it has to be his, but he probably won't believe me. I really do think we should tell him. Tonight, after the show."

"Fuck no. We are not telling him tonight. We are not telling him tomorrow. We'll tell him after we get back to LA." Callum grabs his ponytail and yanks it in frustration. "I'm serious, Becka. We can't tell him until after we get back to LA."

"Cal, then he'll call me a liar. He might stop loving me, thinking I lied to him." I sigh for effect, giving Dom his cue. I knew Cal would come at me at some point between tonight or tomorrow night. So Dom's been following me around to try to catch us in the act on film.

"Or he'll see you for what you really are. A cheater," he snarls. "This thing between us. It never should have happened. I'll support the baby, and you, of course. We'll talk about it when we get back to LA," he reiterates again. "We'll need to think of a way to let Mav know." His Adam's apple bobs with another hard swallow.

"Oh, fuck. Excuse me. I didn't realize anyone was in here." Dom walks into the bathroom, shooting a side-eye at me as he tucks his chin to his chest. That's my signal. "Becka. Cal." He nods curtly as he continues into the restroom.

"That's okay. We're done here. Right, Becka?" Cal gives me a hard, steely look.

I bite my bottom lip and nod. "Right."

"I'd never purposely horn in on you getting some, Cal, but aren't you about to go on?" Dom looks at his expensive watch, selling this chance meeting. Did I know Callum was going to pull me into the bathroom? No. Did I suspect he'd want some pre-show sex? Yes. I just hope Dom caught what I needed him to.

Callum grabs my hand. "Come on, Becka. Let's go." He starts leading me to the bathroom door.

"Oh, wait. You forgot your phone." Dom grabs my phone off the counter and slyly hands me two.

"Oh, um, thanks." I don't make eye contact with him as I take the phones and slip them into my small crossover bag. I don't need Callum to be suspicious.

As soon as we're clear of the bathroom, I jerk my hand from Callum's. I have to keep up appearances that we aren't together until the band is on stage. But when the Rebels do go on tonight, I'll be editing the movie Dom just made and releasing it with my burner account to the world. Hearts will break, but songs will be written about me.

Epilogue: Carla Dufraine's Rock & Metal Round-up

Breaking News: Blind Rebels Singer Attacks Guitarist on Stage

Several social media sources are reporting that Mavrick Slater, frontman for the Blind Rebels, stopped singing at the beginning of their long-anticipated Madison Square Garden show. Multiple videos from various angles show that while the confused band continued to play, Slater ran across the stage, catching his still playing guitarist Callum Donogue in a flying tackle, taking him all the way to the stage floor.

Videos show the singer straddling his guitarist while he was down and continually punching him, while his twin brother Killian looked on in horror.

Crew members rushed on stage and pulled the singer off the guitarist and dragged him off the stage. Callum's brother, Killian, helped the guitarist to his feet and assisted him off stage, leaving drummer, Sammy Denton, the lone Rebel.

Sammy grabbed Mav's discarded microphone and said,

"Um, sorry about that," before also being escorted from the stage.

A stagehand later returned, announcing that everyone was okay, but the show was over, and audience members should ask for refunds from their ticket seller.

I've contacted the Rebels' representation, but so far, no one has returned my inquiry. Rumor has it, that minutes prior to taking the stage, Slater saw the recently released sex tape of his fiancée, Becka Morrison, in a compromising position with his guitarist in a restroom. Rumors also say that Becka is pregnant with Donogue's child. The Rebels' camp is keeping tight-lipped about the whole encounter.

We will post again as soon as we know more. Keep rocking!
– Carla.

FIND *out what happened to each member after the break-up in the* Blind Rebels *series available on Amazon and in Kindle Unlimited.*

Part Two

Blind Rebels Extras

Chapter 34

Kady's Words- From Bridging the Silence

Killian

Today was heavy and I'm ready to get the hell out of Mav's house and just veg for a while. It was the kind of day where the emotions and feelings exhausted me and even though I haven't done much physically, I need to hit the road and get home. I'm not used to feeling like this unless Cal's involved. We've been connected since before birth. It's really draining to try to keep something from him. But it's not a Cal thing this time.

Sammy and I are going surfing up the coast tomorrow. I don't know who needs it more this time. Me or him. I need time in the saltwater bath to wash the sorrow of today away. And cleanse away some of the guilt, both about Kady, for whom I have plenty, and about Sevenya for whom I have mountains.

It's been awhile since we've hit the waves and I need some time in the ocean to right myself. And to think I probably never would have even learned to surf if it hadn't been for Sammy joining the Rebels. Now we can all surf but Sammy and I surf the most out of the four of us.

I grab my suit jacket out of Mav's entry closet, hoping to slip out unnoticed but that's not my luck today. Kady and Mav stand at the door, waiting to say goodbye I guess.

Kady approaches me and pulls me into a hug. This alone is weird. She hasn't impressed me much as a tactile person. Especially not with me. Of course, I haven't given her much of a reason to be. Being here was my way of apologizing for being a dick to her. For stirring up shit with the band and her, especially between Mav and her. Her chin rests on my shoulder near my ear.

"Thank you for being here." Her voice is a hoarse, raspy whisper with hints that at its full strength it might be velvety. I pray that these aren't her first words. Because those should belong to either Mav or Hayleigh- definitely not me. I don't deserve them.

"*You* were here, Killian. Not just physically because Mav asked you to be, but emotionally. I saw that." She squeezes me a little tighter to her. "I see you, Killian. *You.* I don't know what is holding you down, what you feel so bad about, but I know it's not just the thing between us." She takes a quiet breath.

"Let your friends help you with those secrets that you're keeping or they might pull you under with them."

She squeezes my shoulders to her as I nod because now I'm the one who can't speak. She's not just speaking, which is cause enough to celebrate, but she's speaking to my heart. She's somehow figured me out, despite knowing me last, and despite the fact that I've given her little reason to even trust me, let alone want to know or interact with me.

"You're a good guy but for some reason you hide that. Let the nice guy out sometimes, Kill. I know he's in there."

I nod again and she pulls away and looks at me, staring into my soul as if I was that transparent.

My eye contact with her is brief because I can't hold it. Somehow this woman knows that the secrets I hold are dark ones despite me putting in all of my energy to keep them at bay. How she knows I hold onto a secret that could probably destroy the band and enough guilt that it could drown a man I am not sure. Somehow Kady's figured out they exist when no one else knows, not even my twin. Especially not my twin.

I do the only thing I can do right now and that's walk out of this house and head back to my own.

Sammy

My best friend leaves and I can't believe he's *still* being so fucking rude to Kady. I thought Kill was over that shit. Fighting the urge to go after him and tell him to quit being such a damn dick, I turn towards Kady and Mav, who stand before me. Kady's probably tired from everything about the day. The memorial vigil was emotional, and she was unsettled when we all got back to Mav's place. That in turn unsettled Mav, who just wanted to console her. But she needs to be ready to receive that and something tells me she not.

"I'm sorry he's so rude. I'll talk to him." I pick up my duffle bag. I need to stick close to Killian. Something's up with him.

"It's time I stay with Kill for a while anyway, instead of taking advantage of Mav."

As I go to leave, Kady approaches me for a hug. There have been a few times that I've touched her in passing when she wasn't expecting it and it startles her. I've tried to school myself not to be touchy-feely with her because it's important to me that she be comfortable with me. I have a feeling she's going to be around us all for a long time, and I don't want her to feel on guard with me.

I've learned just by being around her though, that when Kady offers you that physical connection you take it. It's not something she does often. I open my arms and let her take the lead.

She pulls me into her. "Sammy," she starts, and I blink for a moment, wondering if I imagined it. Was I seriously hearing her speak?

My heart leaps into my throat, almost choking me off, as her rough whisper continues. "Thank you for coming today. You're the nicest and most genuine person I've ever met. You're the glue that holds these guys together. Even they know it."

"I knew you'd get your voice back. I knew it." I hold back the sob that bubbles just under the surface in me, because Mav is no doubt watching our exchange. And Mav is not good with emotion. Hell, I don't think any of us really are.

"Thank you for being you, Sammy." She gasps slightly and allows me to hold her a little tighter. This is the closest she's ever let me get to her. She quakes against me but whether that's from holding in sobs, the raw nerves from the day, or the fact that she's actually consciously vocalizing I'm not sure. "Thank you."

I shake my head slightly. "No. Thank you for getting through to Mav. He needed that trust you put in him."

She squeezes me again at my words and then releases me as Cal starts to approach the door.

I let her go and turn to Mav. "Uh, I'll call you tomorrow Mav." My voice betrays my emotions causing Cal to give me a quick questioning look. But before he can get to me, I snap up my duffle bag and head out to my jeep.

Callum

I approach Kady and Mav as Sammy starts down the walk to his Jeep.

"I'm gonna head out, Kades." I open my arms out to her so

she can clearly see my intention to hug her. She's fairly skittish when it comes to physical contact, and I don't want to bring up any unwanted memories. Especially not on a day like today, the anniversary. I can only imagine on a day like today the memories are not just heavier but fresher. She's cried a lot today. Which is a testament to how much Mav loves her because he's been there holding her every time the tears came. I'm betting neither of them will get much sleep tonight.

I'm surprised when she latches onto me tightly, so I rock her back and forth slightly.

"You need anything, and I mean anything, you text me." My words are spoken quietly into her hair. She may be Mav's girl, but I love her like a sister, and I want her to know she can come to me like she'd come to an older brother. That I'm here for her independently of her relationship with Mavrick.

"Okay." Her strained whisper sounds almost painful as she says the single word. I want to pull her from me and look her over. To make sure she understands what she just did. And then it settles on me, why Kill just left without a word to anyone. What Sammy seemed choked up about as he was leaving. Kady's talking. *Holy shit.* It might just be a coarse whisper but she's fucking talking.

I don't know what to do with this. I want to make a big deal about it. I want her to know how amazing it is to hear her voice. About how Mav is right-- that she is fucking brave as he says to her repeatedly. But I also don't want to single her out or embarrass her either.

"Cal." The ways she says my name almost brings me to damn tears. "Callum, you're like a brother to me. No. More than a brother to me. Much more. Thank you for coming today. For always just being there. Here."

"Anything. Anytime. Especially for you." My own words are a rough whisper clogged with emotion. I seem to be full of them lately.

"You," she gasps a little bit. "You are a great dad. Gibson is a happy, bubbly baby because you give him exactly what he needs. A dad. A role model. You are giving him yourself and that's exactly what he needs. Don't stop doing that. And let the guys and me help you when you need it because you are exactly what he needs."

She squeezes me to her tighter and I reciprocate. She just gave me the best gift ever with those words. Even better than the pictures she took that now hang in various areas of my house.

"Kady," I can't even complete my thought because it's that much. Between watching Kady come apart all day while Mav held her together, to her fucking breaking through and talking, to her words. It's all a lot of damn feels and I'm not used to having to deal with all these emotions, especially not all at once.

"Go home and give him a big hug from me. I'll see him soon." She squeezes my shoulders.

"You bet I will, and we'd both like that." I say quietly while I hug her to me one more time.

Over her shoulder I can see Hayleigh and Harden gathering. Hay has a suspicious look on her face. I pull back from Kady and clear my throat.

"Take care. See you soon Kady. Mav- I'll be in touch for those beers you owe me." I make eye contact with him so he knows that Kady's talking. I have a feeling he already knew he owed me beers but he definitely owes me some now that he let Kady drop it like that on each of us.

I shake Harden's hand and give Hayleigh a quick squeeze to say goodbye and then head home to my son.

Chapter 35

Original Chapter 1 of Blending Chords- Callum

My head gives the tight, achy throb of an early morning on little sleep and no coffee. The shave I need will have to wait, again, because Gibs is awake even though he shouldn't be.

I offer him a baggie of cereal as he settles into my lap. But he's not that interested in the Cheerios. Instead, he leans back against my chest, like he's done since he was an infant, and gazes at the TV filled with the bright colors of some cartoon on mute.

His eyes partially close and his head dips forward. He jerks up with his eyes open and arms flailing. Then settles back in with a whimper.

"You sleepy buddy? Daddy sure is." He shakes his head, tossing it back and forth against my chest, then arches his back. I kiss his soft, blonde curls. He sure didn't get this hair from me, that's all from his mom.

As he reclines back against me, I stroke my thumb along his leg and hum. This tune isn't a nursery rhyme. It's not even a song, not yet. It's something we were tossing around yesterday afternoon before the gig, but the guitar parts are just not coming together the way they usually do. I can't get them right. I hum it over and over, a riff building in my mind. I'd give anything to grab my guitar and work it out. But my music room isn't childproof. Plus, I'm praying he'll drift off to sleep for a few more hours soon.

My notebook. I'll just jot this down before I lose the music. It's on the table in the entry. Trying not to disturb Gibs who's not quite asleep but not quite awake either, I stand us up to grab it.

Once he senses the movement, Gibson grabs hold around my neck hard and starts to whine something that sounds a lot like no. I flip open my notebook and scrawl out some notes, but the idea is already evaporating. My brain is so tired nothing sticks anymore.

Since he's not interested in sleep, the cheerios, or cartoons I decide that maybe I can sneak in a shave or even shower.

Stopping by his room, I gather some of his favorite toys and toss them on the blanket I've spread on my bathroom floor. Gibs starts pushing around his favorite blue truck so I pull my razor and shaving cream from the drawer. I don't even get shaving cream over my whole face when little hands pull at the legs of my sweatpants, nearly pulling them down.

"Up, Dadda! Up!" He starts crying while continuing to tug on my pants. I'm not even sure I got all the shaving cream off my face.

"Dadda," He whines from my bed while I put on the same clothes I wore yesterday and possibly even the day before.

I'm pretty sure his back teeth are finally coming in. Either that or God is punishing me. Possibly both.

"Open for daddy, bud?" I try sticking my pinkie finger in his mouth, but he turns his head, lips clamped shut in a tight frown. All I get is a pitiful moan. If I force the issue he'll probably bite me. Again. It's hell when pieces of sharp enamel are busting through your tender gums.

"Okay, you win, bud. I'll leave your mouth alone." I tousle his hair.

We head back to the living room and he resettles on my lap, resting his back against me. He takes control of the small baggie of Cheerios and soon his soft munching vibrates through his head and into my chest. I lay my head on the back of the couch and close my eyes just for a minute.

The sensation of falling has me jerking head up, suddenly and completely alert.

"Fuck!"

I scan the room, arms flailing in panic as I pat the area around me, like that'll find him. Because clearly, my two-year-old son slipped between the cushions of my dark gray leather couch.

A familiar deep, rumbling chuckle has me turning my head to find Mav, our lead singer, standing in my kitchen sipping from my favorite mug. He watches me, his eyebrow cocked as amusement lifts one side of his mouth in a smirk.

"Good afternoon, Sleeping Beauty." He chuckles again and takes another sip out of my cup. He's purposely goading me.

"Gibs—" My heart pounds harder— I don't see or hear my son.

Mav nods his head towards the sliding door. His wife Kady is helping Gibson fill and pour out cups of sand in the green, turtle-shaped sandbox outside.

My eyes land on the clock on the wall behind Mav's head. It's nearly one in the afternoon!? No way have I been sleeping for almost seven hours, sitting upright on a couch? That can't be right.

"Sammy and Kill left to get food, they should be back in a few." Mav joins me in the living room, sitting in the chair across from me, his legs crossed at the ankles while looking at me with judging eyes.

"You look like crap, Cal." Just what everyone loves to hear

when they first wake up. My already grumpy mood just got worse.

"How long have you been in my house?" I can't help my scowl.

"Me? Since eleven-ish." He watches me expecting a reaction. Who does he think he is, Dr. Phil?

"Sammy got here about eight. Found you sound asleep on the couch with Gibson crawling around on the floor with his truck." Mav looks me in the eye, concern banding across his forehead.

"This is the last straw, Cal." He shakes his head at me. "We decided to wait until you woke up naturally since you've been such a ray of fucking sunshine lately."

I probably slept more this morning than in the previous week. Yet I'm still so dog-tired I'm not firing on all cylinders yet.

"I'm—"

"Exhausted, we know." He sets my mug on my table without a coaster. "It's why we're here. Consider this your intervention."

My back straightens. Intervention? They can't possibly think I'm using. They *know* I haven't touched the hard stuff in a long time. Way before Gibson.

Mav chuckles again. "Kady'll do the main presentation. After we eat." He slaps my back and stands as Kill and Sammy walk in holding In-n-Out bags. "You'll be more agreeable on a full stomach."

"Finally woke up, didja?" Sammy sets down a carrier of drinks on the dining room table. "Come eat."

Kill opens the sliding door, "Food's here, Kade. Cal's awake." He hooks his head toward the dining table as he turns back towards it.

Kady wipes the sand off her legs. It's only now that she stands that you can see the round to her abdomen. I remember when Becka started to show with Gibs, and rage starts bubbling the acid in my stomach.

When Kady picks Gibson up he squishes his hands together on her cheeks forcing her to make a fish face. "Kaykay! Ishy!"

He lays his head against her shoulder as she brings him in. An intimate gesture that exacerbates the building anger.

He's usually eaten by now, so I meet Kady at the open door. I hold my hands out to Gibs and the little traitor clutches her around the neck and screeches "No! KayKay!"

"I got 'im." She smiles and pats his butt. "Diaper and then lunch, right Gibs?" He nods against her neck but doesn't release his grip on her.

"You, eat." She sends me a sharp look and nods at the table. They return a few minutes later all smiles.

I pick at my fries while Kady helps Gibson eat his lunch. Mav slips him one of his fries and Gibs joyfully grabs it and shoves it in his mouth.

"Mav," Kady chastises. "You know Cal doesn't want him eating fried stuff."

Her husband leans back in the chair with his 'whatchya gonna do about it' smile and sets another fry onto Gibs' tray, which Kady promptly intercepts before Gibs notices it.

"Quit being an instigator." She swats at him then wipes my munchkin's face before pulling him out of his highchair. "Eat up guys, band meeting in ten to twenty, depending on how long it takes me to get him down."

It's not right that Kady's more of a mother to Gibson than his own mom. Not. Fair.

"You should eat, you heard Kady." Sammy eyes my burger.

I pick the onions off and polish it off before Kady returns, knowing if I don't Sammy will devour it.

"Let's move this to the music room." Kady herds us down the hall. She may be our newest member but she's also the bossiest. I wonder if Mav regrets asking his wife to be a Blind Rebel.

Mav immediately flops in my chair, my coffee cup back in his hand.

"Get out of my chair." My clenched jaw makes it sound mean. But he's still trying to provoke me and it's starting to work.

"I thought you'd be less of a jerk since you got some sleep and food." He stays in my chair.

When he's slow to get out I push the back of the chair up until he tumbles out, landing on the nearby couch next to Sammy.

Kady stands, hands on her hips, in front of me. "This is an emergency band meeting slash intervention, Cal."

"Look, I don't know what you think I've been doing, but I swear to you I'm clean. I haven't—"

"I told you he'd think we were talking drugs, fifty bucks! Pay up, suckers." Sammy jumps up and sticks out his hand to the other members collecting his money. Everyone grumbles and shoves money at him. Even Kady.

Why do I get the feeling this dressing down is going to hurt?

"We love you. We're a family before a band. But you're a walking zombie lately and a cantankerous one at that. We'd usually tolerate it but your work is suffering. We're trying to finish this album. We depend on your songwriting and you're just not gelling." Mav blows out a breath.

He's trying to choose the right words. Words I won't instantly reject. I clench my hands into fists. I'll come out swinging if I have to.

"We get it- Gibson's your life." He motions at the baby monitor. "We'd be the first ones all over you if you weren't putting him first." He pauses and glances at the other members.

"Dude, we all see it. You're beyond spent. You've lost weight. You're writing is subpar. And I'm pretty sure you're wearing the same clothes you wore yesterday. You sure smell like it anyway."

He leans back. "If you keep this up Cal, you'll end up in a

hospital. What good will you be to Gibson then? Seriously." Mav reaches forward and pats my knee. "We're worried, man."

I scan the four pairs of eyes looking at me and I'm overwhelmed at the love and genuine concern on their faces, but I'm also livid.

They aren't single parents. I've been walking this frayed tightrope for two fucking years now without a net. This lifestyle isn't conducive to being the musician I am, the dad I want to be, or the dad Gibson deserves. I drop my head into my hands, my eyes burning at the thought of quitting the band I helped build.

Kady sits on the arm of my chair, hand on my shoulder. It'd almost be easier if I knew they didn't care. If I didn't care about letting them down, letting Gibson down. I care *too* much and that is what's slowly killing me.

"We're not judging, Cal. You're a good dad." Her voice is soft and tender as her hand squeezes my shoulder.

"Ha!" I scoff. If that's the case, I wouldn't have fallen asleep with my toddler on my lap and they wouldn't be here.

"Dude, you need help." My twin cuts right to the chase. "We're not the Blind Rebels without you. Buck up buttercup and hire a manny."

Sammy snorts at Kill. "Dude, a manny is a man-nanny!" He lets out a hearty laugh. "That'll be the day, a strange dude taking care of Gibson. Over Cal's dead body."

Kill slaps Sammy upside his head.

"I've been researching," Kady starts, shooting them a look, before looking back at Mav. He reaches over and rubs her bump.

"There's an agency we're going to use. They fully vet and bond their employees. They take your requirements and match you with possible nannies. This place comes highly recommended."

I shake my head. I can't sluff my son onto a stranger. It's not fair to him.

She frowns and pats my arm. "I know you don't want an outsider watching Gibs. But Cal, this is the perfect time to bring on a live-in. Get a feel for them before we tour. This way, you're not leaving Gibs alone with someone until you're comfortable." I sigh out loud and her pinched expression tells me she heard the frustration behind it. We've had this discussion before.

"Make a stipulation they be available for touring. It's what we're doing." She gives me a sad smile. "You need someone in place. We have the mini tour coming up. And then the summer tour for the album release." Like I need the reminder.

Mav stands and stretches. "Quit being a martyr Cal. This gives you plenty of time to find someone."

"You'll interview them. Make sure they work well with Gibs. You let 'em know *your* rules. Like no fried foods, or no falling asleep when watching cartoons with Gibs."

He glares at me, pissed I fell asleep on Gibs. So, I nodded off. I can't be the first parent in history to fall asleep holding their kid.

I glare right back. He's such a jerk. When he's a dad, then maybe he'll understand. But not really, he's got Kady. Gibson and I have no one.

Kady rests a hand on my arm. "This comes from a place of love, Cal. From all of us." The way she stresses *all* breaks my resolve against help.

They don't understand what it's like to rely on someone only to have them turn around and leave you no matter what you do to appease them. Well, Kill gets it because he's been there. But he doesn't have a kid and wants nothing to do with his nephew.

On one hand, they're right. I've needed help for a while. Between Gibson and the band, I'm wrung dry. Aunt Sandy does what she can but she's older and shouldn't be traveling the country with a rock band. She doesn't deserve our kind of debauchery.

She also needs a life that doesn't include raising yet another kid that's not hers. Kill and I vowed to give her that life. We owe her for stepping up for us.

But trusting someone, let alone an outsider, when everyone else walks out? I don't want that kind of hurt for my son.

"What do I have to do?" Kady winces for a second before realizing what I'm asking.

"I'll get it all set up. I can even help with the interviews. If you want," She bubbles uncharacteristically with excitement.

"Yeah, I'd like that." I swallow and nod. "Thanks."

Mav claps me hard on the back. "Alright, Sleeping Beauty, let's try to make some music!"

Chapter 36

Gibson's Kidnapping from Killian's POV

Cal's been distracted for the last hour and it's bugging the ever-loving shit out of me. I huff my bangs out of my eyes in exacerbation. We're working on music, prepping for another album. But he keeps checking his damn phone instead of staying in the moment. I can't be the only one noticing this shit. I purposely strum an off note. Everyone looks over at me. Everyone except Cal.

He's worried about Ari. The concern sits in the acidy pit of our stomach, churning. If this is what *love* is, I don't want it. Don't need it. There was a time I thought I knew what love was. But I was a stupid kid then. My brother's found his love in Ari and that's great for him. But it's not for me.

I huff again and shift in the chair waiting for someone, anyone but me to call him out. We need his attention back to where it's supposed to be, on the music. I mean, I like Ari and all, and I know he loves her, and she loves both him and Gibs right back. It's the real thing. We all spent last tour inside of their relationship bubble, but this is too much.

About damn time. He sets his phone down and looks up at

us. "Uh where were we?" His mind is still on her and on Gibson.

"We were at the second chorus." Kady smiles at him. "You okay?" He nods and picks right back up where we were. Finally.

We work through the song and when we're done, I consider sharing the song I started writing last night on my own.

Stick with the bass, Kill. It's what you know. Mav's words from the last time I shared a song ring loud in my head as if he said them to me yesterday and not 6 years ago. I can't not write music. I might not be very good at it, but it's how I get out the emotions I can't let myself feel any other time.

"Anyone got something to go with this?" Sammy thrashes out on his drums. I pluck a beat along with him just making it up as I go, and Mav starts bobbing his head. Kady brings in some piano quickly and soon Mav is humming along and scribbling in his notebook. This is how it happens; it works when we all work together. Cal chimes in and soon we have a workable song. The lyrics aren't quite right yet, but it's coming together.

Sammy stands up and stretches from behind his kit, his t-shirt pulling up at his midsection. Kady throws him an orange sports drink. "Sorry Sam, we're out of the red ones."

"No worries. This is good." He cracks it and downs half of it before sitting back down.

"Okay look, I think I have it now. Check it." Mav starts to sing the part that was bothering him acapella.

"That's the shit." Sammy nods in agreement. We all turn towards Cal, wanting, needing his opinion on Mav's newly shaped lyrics. But his head is bent down futzing with that damn phone of his again.

This is getting fucking ridiculous.

I want to tell him, but my heart starts racing, and I feel the need to run, to get away, all while the acid in my stomach starts to bubble up my throat. *I need to hide when I haven't hidden in years.* Get the fuck out of here, away from *him.* But who the fuck is *him?*

I scan the room frantically trying to figure out what the fuck is going on, because what my eyes are seeing does not make sense with the way I feel. I'm suddenly fucking petrified. But it's not me. And it's not Cal. I try to draw in a breath.

Bad man. Bad man. Bad man. A green balloon. Bad man. Green balloon. Ari crying. Aiden motionless on a lawn. Gibs? It's Gibs. Oh fuck. It's Gibson.

I look at my brother. He doesn't know. But he does. Shaking, I grab his arm and squeeze tight, causing his head to snap towards me and away from his phone at last.

"Gibs." It's all I can pant out as the panic seizes my chest, closing off my breath. But he knows, deep down he has to know it's all wrong. My head spins with fear coming from both Callum and Gibson.

The color from his face slowly drains as the phone in his hand starts ringing.

"What?" He spits out, but his eyes never leave me. His panic joining mine as his heart races just behind mine.

"What the fuck do you mean they're gone?" His loud voice catches the attention of the others and if they had no idea what was going on before, they know now something is gravely wrong. "How the fuck do you lose the only two fucking people you're supposed to be keeping safe? You're fired. Immediately."

Lost? Gibson and Ari are lost? No wonder I feel like this- he's terrified. Gibs is fucking terrified. I rock in the seat as his fear becomes my fear. He wants Callum. He doesn't understand what's happen. *Daddeeee. Dadddeeee.* How am *I* feeling this and not his own fucking father? Unless Cal is blocking him out. Maybe it's part of being a dad, having to block out that connection to your kid.

My brother stands up, still staring at me, then down at my hand still squeezing the fuck out of his arm. Everyone else in the room stands up in unison and starts moving like a well-oiled machine. Mav is on his phone talking in hushed but firm tones, Kady is trying to redirect my brother, and Sammy has his hand out towards Callum.

"I'll drive you and Kill." He wants the keys to the SUV. Callum pulls them out of his pocket and puts them in Sammy's hand. He's so fucked he can't drive. That's not Callum. We all walk out to the front of the house.

"We're right behind you," Mav says as he opens the door to his Corvette and Kady slides into the side. I glance up at the house, the Slater's nanny stands at the window watching us leave, clutching Brio to her in a tight hug.

Acid keeps waving up my throat, wanting me to expel it. I don't know if this is from Cal or Gibs or some sort of sick combination of both. I don't know that Cal understands that I'm somehow connected to Gibson. Is this new or have I always been this way but it'd been blocked when I cut Gibs out of my life when he was born. I only recently started loving him and now look, he's in trouble and is really scared.

Before the car even stops, Callum is out the door and trotting across the park, towards Jax.

"What the fuck?" Cal changes direction and charges forward towards Aiden, who's sitting on a bench his head in his hands.

"Calm the fuck down Callum. Jumping Aiden won't help." Jax holds Callum back from taking Aiden apart with his bare hands, because he wants to. We all know it. You don't fuck with family and Gibson's the closest family we have.

"Where's my son, Jax? It's his fucking job to know. I pay him to protect them." He points at Aiden over Jax's shoulder as he continues to be a barrier between Cal and Aiden. "Where the fuck are they, Aiden? What the hell happened?"

Sammy walks the perimeter of the park in one direction. Mav does the same in the other direction. Kady consoles Aiden, while Jax continues to restrain my brother. Everyone is looking for Gibson. But I can't.

I drop to a worn bench on the opposite side of the playground as Aiden. I can't catch my breath. Callum's lack of breath chokes me. But mostly, I close my eyes and hope to feel my nephew again. I concentrate, trying to separate Callum's distress against that faint feelings of Gibson, but fuck if I can feel it now and that freaks me more than anything.

The pressure, the stress on Callum, it's all too much and I can't hold it in any longer. I lean over and throw up onto the grass next to me. Mav and a police officer walk towards Callum and our stomachs drop simultaneously. Fuck this doesn't look like good news.

"You okay, Kill?" Kady's tentative voice shatters me. We've mended our bridges, Kady and me. But she's still cautious around me, even now. I can't let that get to me. Not right now.

I just look at her and shake my head. I'm not okay. My twin is not okay. My nephew is fucking terrified. Off who knows where with who knows who, he's not okay either. Nothing about this is okay.

"We'll find him, Kill." She lays a reassuring hand on my shoulder, like she was doing with Aiden minutes ago.

The police gathered with Callum and Mav disperse and Callum drops to his knees. His anguish is my anguish. His heart tears with mine. He's desperate for Gibson and no one understands this. He's unsure of Arista. Did she do this? In his heart he doesn't think it's possible that Arista did this, but then did she? The cops seem pretty convinced she did.

R

GRETA SETS a sandwich down on the table next to me, but I can't even think about eating it. Not when we don't know anything. The cops made us come back home in case there was some sort of ransom call, or they just come home. Everyone is here. Everyone sits quietly, in their own head with the TV on in the background on mute, cops milling around.

We all jump every fucking time Cal's phone goes off. He answers it on the first ring each time, growing more and more agitated with each call from the media. How the fuck they managed to get his number again I have no idea. Kady eventually takes his phone and goes into his office with it, promising to answer each call. He doesn't want her to take his phone. He wants to be the one to answer *the* call, but he doesn't have it in him to argue with her.

Cal grows more despondent as each hour passes; his feelings sit heavy in my stomach. His worries about Gibson paramount, his questioning of Arista's motives grow and it all churns in me. It's fucking scary as my twin, my other half, goes deeper and deeper into the pool of darkness, just like the sun that sinks past the horizon.

Sammy grabs my shoulder as he walks behind me. He's been pacing the house but trying not to pace. A worried Sammy needs to move. He loves Gibson and Ari too. As do Mav and Kady. I love him too. Our relationship has been growing stronger this last year. I don't know that Cal even realizes that I love his son.

Greta tries handing Cal a bottle of water, but he rejects it.

"You should at least drink something," Mav says to him. "Don't get dehydrated."

My twin's jaw tightens, and he shakes his head. He wonders if Gibson's hungry or thirsty. He's angry at Mav and wants to curse him out. But he's also grateful he's here. Thankfully Mav doesn't push the subject because I think if he did, Cal would snap.

The house grows quieter, everyone stuck in their own head as it grows even darker outside. The sound is the murmur of the police officers sitting at the breakfast bar.

Cal's thoughts darken even further as he bites his lip hard. His thoughts come through clear and they both disturb and sicken me. *I'd gladly let them kill me if whoever has him could guarantee my baby's safety.* What the fuck, Cal? You can't seriously be thinking of that. Of dying. Of leaving us all. Of leaving me.

He could be with my brother and be fine and that would be enough for me. I'd trade my life for his because fuck, my baby hasn't lived long enough.

"No!" I yell, louder than I mean to. All eyes are on me now. Officers move closer, the sound of their hands unsnapping their tasers from their belt. But I pay it no mind as I glare at my brother, so he knows I know what he just thought. Why would he put that energy into the world with those kinds of thoughts? "Don't fucking think like that, asshole."

I grab the pillow from the couch and chuck it at him and then run upstairs. I need distance from Cal and all this churning negativity. These feelings aren't doing anyone any good. Especially not Gibson. The further I get away from Cal the more I feel Gibson. He's faint, but his fear claws at me, like a spider monkey climbing a tree. His exhaustion tires me. His hunger takes me to the past, to times when Cal and I were hungry.

I don't dare tell Cal any of this because I don't believe it myself. How can *I* feel him? He's not my son. Does Cal feel this? Is that why he's thinking those kinds of thoughts. Thoughts of dying, of wanting to die to save his son.

"Kill," Sammy says quietly as he puts his hand on my shoulder. I should have known he'd follow me up here. "You okay?"

I just shake my head, my chin to my chest. I can't tell him what Cal was thinking. They're his private thoughts. But Sammy knows where my distress stems from, that it comes from the unusual connection that I share with my brother and apparently my nephew too. I especially can't tell him he's thought like this before, only instead of Gibson he was saving it was me.

Sam pats my back hard. "They'll find him, man. Don't worry. They've got to find him." He squeezes my shoulder before letting go and follows me to the room I use on the rare occasions I sleep here. I throw myself across the bed face down. The further away I am from my brother the harder it is to feel his exact thoughts. I can still feel his moroseness but not his exact thoughts.

Sam slides down my footboard so that he's sitting on the floor, leaning against my bed. He's mostly quiet, but every once in a awhile there is a hitch in his breathing that makes me think he's not as okay as he's projecting.

"If something happens to Gibson, I don't think Cal will make it." His words are a hitched whisper because he too doesn't want the world to have that energy. I don't think he meant to say them out loud. But he's right. When Gibson came into the world, Cal's purpose, his world shifted. If he loses that purpose...I shudder thinking of the Cal before Gibson.

My own despair at the thought of what could happen if Gibson is hurt or worse mixes with that of my brother's downstairs.

Who has Gibson, and why? And what the fuck are they doing to him right now because little man is scared. I feel it vibrating through him.

I don't know how long we're upstairs, sitting in silence. But it's solidly dark outside now. Sammy's stayed up here with me because for whatever reason he doesn't want me to be alone.

"We should probably head back downstairs, yeah?" He pushes himself up off the ground but not with his usual gusto. When we get to the living room, Sammy slides onto the floor near the couch and I flop back down in the seat I was sitting in before, silently making sure that Cal knows I will not be party to anymore thoughts of him dying.

179

Time moves slowly and quickly at the same time. Sammy gets up and walks behind me and squeezes my shoulder again and when I don't respond to him, he ruffles my fucking hair like I'm a kid. He's purposely pushing my buttons. I weave away from him, swatting at his hands.

But he pulls me into a hug. "They *will* find him." He says it quietly but with absolute certainty this time. I shrug him off as the phones and radios of the officers milling about the house start going off simultaneously. Everyone's talking at once and while it's obvious something has happened, it's impossible to tell what that something is because all the voices mix.

An officer approaches my brother. "There's been some developments. We believe your son and fiancée are barricaded inside a house not far from here. But so far, we've been unable to establish communication."

Cal stumbles to his feet as she continues. "We want you at the scene to make a plea over the loudspeaker. We're hoping that will get them to communicate with us, if not surrender."

My brother shoves my nephew's comfort toy, RuffRuff, in his jacket pocket. He won't be coming back without his son. We all move towards the door. The cop stops and turns.

"We can't have any other people on the scene. The rest of you will have to stay."

"He's my twin. I'm coming," I grit out, refusing to take no for an answer. Like hell will I let Cal out of my sight, especially now. My throat feels like sandpaper and like we might both hurl at the same time. "If something goes sideways, he'll need someone there." Sammy squeezes my shoulder tight again.

I hold my hand over my brother's balled up fist in the back of the squad car as we are driven down the hill to the house where Gibson and Ari are. We wind our way through a crowded scene. There are so many people here, I honestly don't understand why the others couldn't come. A few more wouldn't have made a difference.

We are taken to some sort of tactical vehicle that looks like a cross between those armored cars that transport money from businesses and a tank.

"Best we can tell, there are three adults and one child in the house," another officer tells us, he appears to be the one in charge here at the scene.

He hands my brother a radio. "Just let them know you're here, that you want your son and to pick up the phone when it rings. Say nothing else." He nods his understanding.

"This is Callum." His words echo from the speakers on the top of our armored vehicle. "You have my son. I just want my boy back. Please answer the phone. We want to talk." The officer nods and motions for the radio back. But Cal has a special message that he's going to deliver whether the officer says it's okay or not. "Gibs baby. It's daddy. I love you baby. Daddy loves you so much."

The officer snatches the radio from him, a few curses slipping out from his professional cop persona. Someone in the back of the vehicle calls the house. The phone rings and rings on speaker, but no one picks up. *Please pick up. Anyone. Answer the damn phone.*

Cal's considering charging the house himself. He knows I'd be right behind him. And fuck yeah I would, I'd follow him into any battle but especially this one. Messing with my nephew is messing with me, motherfucker. Let's do this.

There's a slight fluttering of a curtain, but that's it. The house remains dark and still from the exterior.

Cal repeats his request on the loudspeaker for the officers a few times, leaving the personalized message for Gibson out.

Officers dressed in tactical gear begin to assemble at the front of the vehicle we're in, their movement highlighted by lights of our vehicle. We look out a window at the house as Callum makes silent pleas for Gibson, only *I* feel them. *Daddy's here baby. Hold on for daddy.*

Outside the truck, SWAT officers seem to be gathering. Cal and I catch a glimpse of a rifle at the same time.

"Fuck no! No guns. He's just a baby. I haven't had enough time with him. I'll go in, not them. Not with guns." He stands pointing at the officers gathering, and tries to make his way out of the armored vehicle we are in. I stand behind him ready to grab him if I need to. If he runs out there the police will detain him, and his son will be in there without his dad out here.

"Don't make me handcuff you to that chair, son," the older cop barks from the rear of the armored vehicle.

Cal's chest puffs up and his patience thins as the tendons in his neck stand out. I grab him around the shoulders to restrain him. He's about to go off, it thrums through us both. The antsy nerves. He wants his son. He needs to see his baby, hold his baby, to know that Gibs is okay.

"They know he's in there. Let them get him back, okay?" I squeeze him like Sammy squeezed me back at the house, trying to reassure him. I eventually let him go, but he's still considering making a run for it. He shifts in his chair, the corners of his mouth pulled down into a deep frown.

"Don't even think about it son." The older cop seems to read Cal's body language as well as I read his thoughts.

"Let me go over how this is going to go down. First, we're going to knock. If that doesn't work after about 15 minutes, we'll fire a flash round into the house. You'll hear that, maybe even see it. Don't be alarmed. It's meant to disorient the captors. It won't be fired into the room with your son. Infrared tells us he's in a room at the back of the house. One of the adults is in the same room with him. The other two are in the front. Once the flash round has been fired through the window, the SWAT team will breach the door. Officer Sanchez here," he points to one of the officers at the rear of the assembled group. "His assignment is to get to your son. That's his only job. Get Gibson and bring him out."

Cal rubs the screen we're watching, giving Officer Sanchez all the strength he has in him to get his baby out safely.

"Who's getting Ari out?" Cal turns and looks at the officer.

"We aren't sure if Arista Addington is an accomplice or a second victim."

"Bullshit is she an accomplice!" *She loves Gibson.*

"We don't know that. She'll be detained and taken to the department and interviewed."

Cal quiets, he's running out of gas. He doesn't know who to worry about more. Gibs or Ari. The cops planted just enough of a seed of doubt in him, to wonder if she had a hand in kidnapping his son. He doesn't know what to do.

Cal jumps under my grip as the first blast of the flash round sounds. One, two, three. All we hear is muffled angry shouts. All we can see are shadows of the police moving around the house through the closed curtains. So instead, we focus on the door now hanging from the hinges. Flashlights move around the room erratically. An officer passes by the doorway with a rifle drawn on someone in the front room.

I can't help my tight hold on Cal's shoulder as he sucks in a desperate breath.

Dammit Sanchez, where are you? Where's my son?

Then Cal audibly gasps as flash of Gibson's blond curls appear just inside the door. He's clutched tightly to the chest of an officer, one hand covering his head, holding it to the officer's vest. The officer jogs down the three stairs and starts across the lawn.

I let go of Cal because he needs to get to Gibson. Gibson needs his dad. The absolute terror pulsing through my nephew about brings me to my knees right here in the armored vehicle. I gasp for breath as he tries to call out to the only solid in his life- his dad. My twin.

I stay in the armored truck, giving Cal and Gibson the space they need. Their immense relief and exhaustion are almost too much, so I sit back down and wait. Until Cal's anger starts bubbling up through me. I'm not sure if this means Gibson's hurt or not, but I need to go to the ambulance to make sure. As I'm crossing the yard, I see her. Fucking Becka, being led out of the house in handcuffs. He sees her too. That's the anger. And Arista's fucking brother-in-law. How the hell do they know each other? I knew I should have popped him at the go-kart track when I had the chance.

When I get to the ambulance, Cal's strapped to a gurney holding Gibson on his lap, shooting death rays at Becka and Todd. He's considering unstrapping himself. I have to get his attention off them and back onto Gibson.

"We'll meet you there, we all will." I hold up my phone, so he knows that everyone back at his house knows that they are good. That they are being taken to the hospital for precautionary reasons, but they are fine.

I go to shut the ambulance door for the paramedic.

"Wait Kill!" My brother's eye contact tells me he's not done here. "Find out about Ari." I nod my promise to him, and the ambulance drives slowly down the crowded street.

R

AFTER HOURS of being poked and prodded, Gibson clutches my brother's neck with a death grip, his fingers wrapped tightly in his dad's hair while Cal tries to fill out the discharge paperwork.

"Here, I'll do it." I take the pen from him and start filling it out despite the looks from Nurse Hatchet behind the desk. My brother turns his attention to Gibson, everyone's stomach growling at the smell of the chicken Kady brought especially for Gibson.

I'm filling out the last of the papers when he taps my foot with his. "I'll be right back." I nod, concentrating on the paperwork in front of me as he wanders off to wherever. I pull my credit card from my wallet. I know damn well my brother will pay me for whatever the fuck this will cost, he'll just want to leave, but I wouldn't care if he didn't pay me.

I sign the receipt they give me and head back into the waiting area. Mav nods at a window where I can see Ari's sister and Callum still clutching his son tightly, with what looks like a doctor. Ari's sister looks like hell, and I'm reminded of the conversation about Ari's condition I had with Officer Sanchez, who came to see how Gibson was doing.

"She was wrapped around that baby, Gibson, in a protective bubble. It took me forever to pull him from her. She didn't understand that I was there to help. She was confused and kept calling me Todd, thought I was going to hurt the baby. I didn't get a great look at her but she seemed to be in rough shape. It was hard for me to leave her there, but I had my orders."

Callum reaches out and squeezes Ari's sister's shoulder and returns to us. He says nothing about Ari's condition, probably because of Gibson in his arms. Gibson, cries in devastation when Callum straps him into his car seat in the back of the SUV because he doesn't like being separated from his dad.

"I'll drive man. Sit back there with him." Mav reassures Cal, who just nods and slips into the backseat with Gibson, his hand on Gibs the whole ride home. Gibson sucks on Cal's finger, something I've never seen him do before. The one time he takes it from him for a second to pull his hair back, Gibson screams for him.

Back at the house, Gibs sits on Callum's lap at the table to eat his chicken. Cal tried to slip him into his highchair, but he screamed like he did in the back of the car. It's a gut wrenching scream that tears at my soul. I've never heard before. I don't think Cal has either. When Kady arrives after us at the house, she hands us our own food from the same chicken place and kisses Gibson goodbye.

"If you need us, call okay?" She hugs Cal who nods at her.

"I will, thanks." He shoves another bite of food in his mouth.

"We're going man, but we'll be back tomorrow bright and early." Mav pats his shoulder and Cal nods.

After they're gone and we've all eaten, Callum takes Gibson upstairs and returns about forty minutes later.

"He finally fell asleep but fought it the whole time." Cal glances up the stairs and then returns his stare at us.

"I need a favor from you two." He looks between Sammy and I.

"I promised Vi I'd be back at the hospital, Ari's been beat to hell, her arm dislocated, broken ribs. She's not waking up. She's in bad shape. Will you both stay with him? I don't know how long he'll sleep. The doctor mentioned he could have night terrors or sleeping problems." He sighs and wonders if he's doing the right thing. If he should leave his son to check on the woman he loves, the woman who probably saved his son from injury or worse.

"We've got him, Cal," Sammy says. "You can trust us."

Cal nods solemnly, his resolve to not leave his son still strong, but his need to find out more about Ari's condition is pulling him back towards the hospital.

"Be safe driving," I stress at my twin. He's wound up about Ari, about Gibson, but he's also exhausted. We all are.

"I will. Text me if he needs me." We nod and he goes, but I feel his reluctance all the way down the street.

Sammy and I flop onto the couch and don't even bother to turn on the TV.

"Fuck," Sammy releases, drawing out his favorite word.

"Yeah."

Sammy pulls up his feet on the couch and eventually dozes off. With nothing but his soft snores for company I let my heavy-lidded eyes shut but they aren't shut but a minute when Gibson wakes.

"DADDDEEEE!" He shrieks. Driven by an urge I'm not used to feeling, I hop over the back of the couch and take the stairs two at a time to get to him. His face is red and his soft blonde curls are plastered to his head.

"Hey buddy." I say softly and sit on the edge of his bed. "Daddy went to go see Ari."

Wrong thing to say apparently because at the mention of Ari, he starts to scream again, babbling something I don't quite understand fully. But something about Ari and owies and a bad man.

"Woah little man. Daddy's with Ari to make sure there's no more bad man okay?" Thankfully this makes him nod, so it was the right answer. He climbs into my lap and hugging me around the neck, his fingers pulling the hairs at the nape of my neck.

He babbles quietly. It's weird because I usually have no trouble understanding him. I'm not sure if he's just tired or what but he eventually lays his head on my shoulder and relaxes with a sigh, his finger going into his mouth. He never sucked his thumb before.

I lay him back down on his little bed, but the minute I separate myself from him to stand, he screams again. Sammy joins me and we both sit with him. Then eventually we lay with him. I can only imagine the sight of us, two full-sized adults, a toddler between us, in a little bed shaped like a green race car.

Chapter 37

Sevenya's Death- Sammy's POV

"Sev—I'm home." I take an immediate right through the living room and walk to what is probably my favorite room in our condo. It's a small round room. The real estate agent called it a bonus room and explained that most people use it as an office or small personal gym because of its odd shape. I'm a drummer so I don't need an office and the condo complex has a rad state-of-the-art gym near the pool, so I don't need my own gym. The minute I saw this room I knew it would be my drum room. I had it sound-proofed even before my sister Sevenya and I even moved in.

My practice kit sits proudly in the center. Technically it was my first real full drum kit. I use it as my practice kit now. My touring kit stays packed away in our storage unit until I need it and a smaller kit sits in our lead singer's in-home studio. But this kit- this kit is my baby. I think about sitting down and just going through our album's set list. But my stomach gives a grumble and I know I need something to eat first. I toss my duffle bag just inside the door and then close it again.

Heading back through our sparse living room, I pause and look around. There isn't that much in here yet. A huge couch that we bought with the money left from the advance from the label that didn't go towards the down payment on the condo. A decent TV. Sev's always adding something she's picked up at one of the thrift stores she frequents. This time it's a black throw pillow on one end of the couch. She's adorned it with different white buttons to add a big heart to the design. My sister is wicked crafty like that. It's definitely her handiwork—it looks just like the purple one on her bed. She should think about setting up a craft table at the downtown market. I know people go gaga over upcycles and her twist on them are awesome. As soon as we get done with this second album, I should have enough saved up so Sev and I can redecorate. Or decorate, rather, since it's so bare I don't think you could call the current state of our living room decorated. I'll let Sev handle that- she has much better tastes.

I'm more about functionality. That sofa is a prime example of functional. It's large enough that three people can sit on it comfortably- hell four could sit on it if they squeezed in. Sev tends to sit in the brown bean bag chair she found at a garage sale tossed in the corner next to the couch. If you glance at it you'd think it was a matched set. She's got such a good eye. My stomach gives another grumble and redirects me to the kitchen at the back of the house. I pass by my kitchen table. Our table, since technically my little sister Sev bought it from a local thrift store. It's big enough that the whole band can sit around including Sev. Who cares that none of the chairs match? Just like the band.

Well, I guess that Cal and Kill kind of match since their twins, although Killian does everything he can to make sure he looks different than his brother Cal. We aren't family by blood, but we are family all the same. It's how I knew we were meant to be a band. It's what will help us make it in this business. We have each other's backs. Always.

189

At the fridge I grab a red Gatorade and slam it down right there in the kitchen.

Then I grab a handful of the gummy bears that Sev always has in the cookie jar on the counter.

Neither of us are the best of cooks but we both have a sweet tooth a mile wide. Our cookie jar is usually filled with candy— buyer chooses the type. Gummy bears are Sev's favorite, so she always chooses them. But I know she doesn't mind if I eat some. Going back for another handful of the colorful bears, I holler back out "Sev? The band's coming over to talk about the shows at the Whiskey. You wanna have tacos with us? Kill's ordering and wants to know."

She probably already knows that Kill's hitting the taco stand. They have been seeing each other for probably about two years now maybe more. They got together a little after we all started living together in that ratty apartment off Sunset. I don't know why they feel the need to sneak around. Yeah, Kill's older than her. Hell, he's older than me. Things between them were a little tense since she got back from her last stint in rehab. But they seem to be as good as ever now. I think Kill just worries she'll fall back into old habits.

But Killian loves my sister and that's all I care about. She needs someone like him. Someone who loves her for who she is and wants only the best for her. He worries about her as much as I do. That's important to me. Sev needs someone watching out for her. So she knows that she's important enough to be worried about. And I think Kill needs someone to fret about.

They are good for each other.

They don't need to sneak around like they do. For whatever reason they aren't comfortable with the whole band knowing they date. Maybe they think Cal would have a problem with it. He might be Kill's twin and the oldest and probably most responsible member of the Blind Rebels. But I don't see him caring about it as long as we are all good. Maybe I should pull Kill aside one of these days and tell him I know. That it's okay. Sev's grown up in this band and views these guys like older brothers, except for Kill.

As I hit the living room, I look at Sev's door. Still shut but I can hear noise from her room.

The radio or maybe her small television. I knock.

"Sev?" Nothing. No stirring behind the door.

Maybe she's in her bathroom. I knock a little harder.

"Hey Sev! You decent? I'm coming in." I turn the knob and it's locked.

"Dammit Sev, open this door." I rest my head on it. Fuck, I hope she's not using again. She worked so hard to get clean, please don't have ruined all that work.

"Sev, I won't be mad. No matter what. Even if you're high. Just open the fucking door."

Still nothing. Not even the harried shuffling of hiding the evidence.

"Sev, I swear I'll break down this fucking door."

I count to three. Still nothing. Using my shoulder, I throw myself against the door until the cheap molding gives way against the equally cheap lock on her door. The smell, a combination of vinegar and urine so thick I can almost taste it, hits me the second I'm in the room. It's the familiar pungent acrid smell of black tar heroin and it turns my stomach. Despite being afternoon, her room is dark thanks to the blackout curtains and it takes a minute for my eyes to adjust.

"Oh Sev." I sigh quietly. "You know I'm going to send you back to rehab, hon." I can't not make good on that promise. The last drug counselor told me I must keep my promises, or she'll never get better. And I always enable her. I have to make good this time. Send her back to rehab or kick her out. Please don't make it come to that Sev. I can't kick you out. You're the only real family I have left.

I don't know how the fuck I'll pay for it, I'm still drowning in debt from her last two stints. But I'll think of something. If I have to take a second mortgage or borrow from the guys. It won't matter. Sevenya will get the help she needs. She'll get through this.

"Sev?" I scan her darkened room until I see the foil on her nightstand. Her arm hanging off the bed, needle dangling precariously just below her elbow.

"Fuck—Sev!" I rush over to her. I yank her from the bed and the needle from her arm falls out. Sev's cold. So cold. Her chestnut brown eyes stare at nothing and her blue lips are opened as if she tried to make a noise. She's rigid and cold. Deep down I know. She's gone but still I have to try. I can't give up on Seven now.

"Fuckin' hell Sev. Wake up." I slap her face gently. No reaction. Not even a blink.

I shake her with one arm as I fumble around her black nightstand for her phone. Finding it I try to call for help but her phone's dead.

"Gotta get a phone. Be right back okay Sev?" I grab the cordless that's hooked to the landline we're required by the condo association to have so that we can buzz people in through the gate.

I dial and head back to Sev.

"911- what is the location of your emergency?"

"9301 Arbor Street, Condo D"

"What kind of emergency?" the disembodied female voice asks. And I don't want to tell her.

"My sister. She's overdosed."

"Is she awake?"

"No."

"Is she breathing, sir?"

"No. I think she might be dead." I don't recognize the shrill pitch of my own voice.

"Dammit Sev. Wake up." But I know it's useless. She's gone. Sev isn't here anymore. The room is void of her spirit. It's too cold and lifeless in here. She took all the life with her. All the sunshine.

"How do you know it's an overdose, sir?"

"The needle was in her arm when I found her. She'd been clean. I thought she was doing good. I thought she was okay." I tell the stranger on the other end of the phone. She probably doesn't care. I just look at Sevenya, dead on the floor next to her platform bed. The platform that Killian built for her.

My chest burns with an intense ache like I've never known. Could it be a heart attack? I could only be so lucky. This happened because of me. Because I wasn't paying attention. I recognized the signs in the back of my mind. Even thought about confronting her. But I fucking put it off.

"Paramedics should be arriving soon. Is your door unlocked? If not, can you unlock and open your door for the paramedics sir?"

"Okay." I leave the phone next to Seven and stumble out of her bedroom and head left to the front door. I fling it open. Mav is standing at the door with his usual smirk, one hand out as if I grabbed the door as he was going to open it. The other with a grocery sack hanging from it.

"Hey fuc—" Mav's words die on his lips as he looks at me. "Sammy?"

"Get out of the way. They'll be here soon." My voice sounds almost robotic. Not like me.

"Who?" His brows pull together as he tries to figure out what's going on. I can't tell him that she's dead.

"The paramedics. Sev—" I can't even get her name out before a huge sob racks through me. I was holding it together. But Mav's here and my sister is dead in her bedroom and the paramedics are pulling up to the curb and suddenly I can't breathe any more. Mav drops the grocery sack on the porch and grabs me as I fall forward. Holding me up by my arms he moves us both inside as the paramedics rush in behind him.

"Where is she?" One barks at me looking around the house. I can only weakly nod in the direction of her room.

They rush in and I follow behind them. It's like being stuck in a really bad dream. Everything is hazy and moving both too slow and too fast. Paramedics rush around her like they're in a time lapsed video.

I only hear certain words. Cold. No heartbeat. No breathing. Rigor. Coroner's office. *Coroner's office.* She's been dead awhile. She's been dead awhile—I should have checked on her before I headed out to the studio this morning to work on the album. Would it have made a difference?

I can't take my eyes off of Sev. Her yellow shirt torn open; defibrillator still attached.

One of the paramedics starts gently removing the electrodes on her chest. He pulls her favorite purple throw blanket off her bed and covers her with it, as if she's just sleeping on the floor and not dead and gone. Another paramedic packs up the other equipment they brought with them and stows it on a gurney. A gurney? I didn't even see it get rolled in here.

"Sir?" One of the paramedics stands in front of me and puts his hand on my shoulder.

"I'm sorry sir, there's nothing more we can do. We've alerted the coroner's office to come. It could take them some time." He looks over my shoulder and addresses Mav. "Is there someone else we can call for you?" The paramedics words are kind and solemn, but my stomach fires up an acidly flare.

I barely make into Sev's attached bathroom. Skidding to my knees, I lift the lid and throw up a colorful kaleidoscope of partially digested gummy bears, swimming in bile into her toilet. Then I heave a few more times before flushing. I don't dare move from this spot, because if I do then it's all too real. Then Sevenya's really dead. Gone.

If I move it means I couldn't fix her. That I failed her.

It smells like her in here. Her strawberry shampoo mingles with the patchouli perfume she always wore. If I stay in this little subway tiled bathroom, Seven isn't laying on the floor of her bedroom. Her favorite plush blanket isn't keeping her life-less body warm. I don't know how long I sit here in front of Sevenya's toilet, but my knees hurt like a motherfucker. But it's nothing like the empty hole in my heart that seems to suck all of the breathable air out of the room like a black hole.

"Sammy?" It's not Mav, but Cal. When did Cal get here? It's not a surprise that he's here. I'm sure Mav texted him. He's our caretaker. The dad to the rest of us. The oldest of the four. His voice sticks with the emotions clogging it. His hand touches my back and rubs a small circle.

"Sammy come on. Let's move out to the couch. It'll be more comfortable." I sit back on my heels and just shake my head.

"Come on man."

"I can't." My voice is so quiet I am surprised when he responds.

"You can. You will. Come on." He reaches a hand over for me to take. He doesn't understand that I can't leave this bath-room. It's not only that I suddenly don't have the energy in me to move, but I can't go through her room to get to the living room. I can't leave her there alone. But I can't sit in there with her either. Because that's not my sister. That's a shell of someone that looks like her. Sevenya's gone but at least in here, in her bathroom it still smells like her. Seven's alive in this room, and in that room she's dead.

When I refuse to take his hand, Cal stands between me and Sev's toilet. He hooks me under the arms and hauls me to my feet.

"Come on, Sammy." Cal moves beside me, his voice low and soft. "Let's go wait on the couch." His arm slips around my waist and he guides me out of Sev's small bathroom and into her room. I don't look over towards her bed by the window. I keep my focus hard on the doorway to the living room.

Killian jogs into the room, panting like he's run all the way from his place, but he stops just inside the door. He looks at me and Cal and then his vision slides over to her bed. To where she lays. To where I can't look.

As if I wasn't broken enough, watching Killian quietly shatter as he sees her motionless body, annihilates any part of my heart that is left. He doesn't move much. His body catches and stills. He takes a deep, ragged breath and then looks over at us. Me being guided by Cal out of the room.

When he turns away from us and towards her. "Suh, Seven..." his voice, barely a whisper, cracks as he talks. "Sevenya?" I can barely hear him.

"No, Sev. Oh Sev." He gasps quietly.

Cal's grip on my waist loosens slightly and he reaches his free hand out to his twin brother. "Kill, let's get Sammy to the couch okay?"

He looks back over at her and then towards us one more time. His breathing labored and his face is whiter than I've ever seen. He nods and quickly moves to my other side and they guide me to the couch. Mav unfolds himself from the floor as the twins deposit me in the middle. He moves into the kitchen and I hear him rifling through the cabinets.

Mav returns and slips a glass of amber liquid into my hand and sits next to me with his arm thrown over my shoulders. He says nothing, just keeps squeezing my shoulder occasionally. I hear an occasional hitching and am horrified when I realize it's me. Crying. Cal sits on the other side of me, hand on my knee. I stare out the opened door but focus on nothing. I pray that I'm having a nightmare. That any moment I'll open my eyes and Sev will be standing over me, hand on her hip. Head tilted to the side, she'll say. "Sammy, you're late."

The amber liquid burns all the way down. I don't know

where Killian's at. I don't see him again until the coroner arrives. He shows up as we all stand when the coroner enters. Kill's face is still pasty and solemn like all of ours. But it's his eyes that kill me. The rims are red and moist, but his actual eyes? They're almost as dead as Sevenya's.

Chapter 38

Meeting Killy-in (Harmony's POV)

"Harmony, hon? Can you come here so we can have a chat?" Miss Shelly asks right when I'm in the middle of drawing a mermaid. I put down the shimmery dark green crayon in my special set and go to Miss Shelly. She opens her arms which always mean she wants to hug me and sometimes it means she wants me to sit on her lap. I give her the biggest hug and she hugs me back even more than normal which is a lot because Miss Shelly hugs are the bestest hugs in the world. Even better from Miss Banterworth at school and even better than the Santa hugs from the Santa at the mall.

Miss Shelly pulls me onto her lap and I lean against her so I can hear her heart and smell her flower perfume. She never wears a different perfume. Always this one.

This is my favorite thing to do, snuggle with Miss Shelly. It makes me calm and feel safe. She says one day I will be too big for snuggles, but I hope I'm never that big.

She tucks my hair behind my ear. "Harmony I love you so much. You know that right?" She looks at me but the corner of her eyes are sad.

"I love you too Miss Shelly to the deepest part of my heart." I don't want Miss Shelly to be sad anymore.

"I love you to the deepest part of mine too, sweet girl." She breathes a heavy breath and buries her nose in my neck. It always tickles when she does that, and I can't help but giggle.

When I stop wiggling because of the tickles, she holds me while I lean on her.

"Tomorrow Drea wants to take you to the big park to meet someone." She tells me while she holds me tight to her still. "Okay?"

I love the big park. There is a pond there with millions of ducks, well maybe not a million but there are a whole lot. And I love to feed the ducks! "Do we got bread I can take?"

"Yes, we *have* bread you can take with you. All the crusts and ends like we always save."

"Yay! The ducks are probably hungry! I hope Miss Drea's friend wants to feed the ducks too."

Sometimes, when I'm running on the path around the pond, I like to pretend a mermaid lives in the pond and she's my real mom. I know it's only pretend...but sometimes pretending makes me happy. Only Miss Shelly knows about my pretend mermaid in the pond though. I don't tell anyone else. Not even Miss Banterworth and she's my favorite person at the whole school.

I don't know why, but I think Miss Shelly is a little sad about me going to the park tomorrow. I snug into her extra tight.

"If you don't want me to go to the park, I can stay with you." I play with the buttons on her sweater. It's her inside the house sweater. She never wears it outside. It's all different colors of blue and has these big fuzzy buttons. I love this sweater. She always has a tissue in the pocket and sometimes a pen.

"I want you to go to the park and have fun with the ducks. I have a meeting tomorrow at the same time. So it works perfect that you go with Drea."

Miss Shelly works at a place where ladies and kids with no houses go when they need help. And she helps them get food and safe places to sleep and stuff like that. It's important to help people when you can. It's how Miss Shelly got me. She was helping my mom when she was pregnant with me, but my mom was really sick and gave me to Miss Shelly and went away to be fixed. She didn't come back. That's why sometimes I pretend she's a mermaid and that's why she didn't come back. But I love Miss Shelly with the deep parts of my heart because I always knowed her.

Sometimes because some of the people need extra help, she has to have meetings when she isn't supposed to work. Also, sometimes she has meetings about me but those are usually with Miss Drea, my social worker. I have one of those because Miss Shelly is not my real mom.

I finish my mermaid picture and then we eat dinner. Miss Shelly made lasagna. That's always my favoritest dinner and she only makes it during the summers or on Saturdays because it takes a lot of steps. Sometimes she even lets me help put it together. I like to lay the noodles down and smear them with the sauce!

Miss Shelly tucks me in, like she always does but her eyes still look a little sad. "Can we read two chapters of Harry Potter tonight Miss Shelly?"

"We can." She pulls out the book off the shelf in my room and snuggles with me on the bed and she reads. I am getting better at reading, but at night I still like it when Miss Shelly reads. She makes all the voices and that's the best. Especially for Harry Potter.

R

"OKAY, HARMONY. HERE WE ARE." Drea lets me out of her car at the big park. We are by the tables. She says I should draw while we wait for her friend to come. I forgot the friend's name but I am surprised that it's a boy!

"I brought you some crayons and paper, I thought you could draw until my friend gets here." She walks us up to one of the tables and I sit in it so I can see the pond. I will draw the pond until her friend comes. I never drawed at the park before.

I start with the ground by the lake and then make some of the plants. I don't know what kind they are. Then I make the blue part of the lake and I make some white and brown dots for the ducks. I know all the best spots that the ducks are at.

Miss Drea stands up. "I think this might be him. You stay here while I check." I just let Miss Drea find her friend. I am busy on my picture.

I hear her say my name so I turn to look at Drea and see her with a man. He's really tall and has longish black hair that sticks out. His shirt and pants are both black and his pants have holes in the knees. His one arm has black and white tattoos, like they are waiting for me to color them all the way down to his hand. The other arm is almost empty of tattoos.

He's staring at me and I feel like he's scared of me even though I'm just a little girl. It's weird that I can almost feel what this man is feeling inside of me. Not like with Miss Shelly- with her I know what she thinks sometimes only because I knowed her my whole life. But I don't even know this man's name and I feel his feelings and he's really scared of me. Silly man.

The man is holding a white teddy bear with a pretty purple bow on his neck and I think he brought it for me. He's squeezing the poor bear so tight that his fluff on the insides might come out.

Miss Drea bends down to me "Harm, hon, this is my friend. He'd like to take a walk with you and talk. Is that okay? Maybe you two can even play if you want."

"Is that for me?" I point to the poor bear, sure that he's going to kill it he's holding it so tight.

"Uh yeah, this is for you." He takes his hand and brushes the bear with it before handing it to me. I hug the bear to me. He smells good. Kind of like the man smells.

"Thanks Mister. Let's go feed the ducks! Drea, can we have the bread?"

Miss Drea hands me the bag of bread I brought. "Go on you two. I'll wait here."

"You can watch Sampson." I give my new bear to Drea. I hear the man make a funny breathing noise and I don't want him to think I don't love the bear because I do. He's my new favoritest stuffed animal I gots. "He needs a nap while we go feed the ducks."

I squeeze the man's hand so he knows it's okay because he still feels a little scared. "Are you ready? The ducks are hungry."

The man and me walk towards my favorite spot for feeding the ducks. All the ducks know it's my favorite spot and they wait there when they see me with my bag of crusts.

But I remember that I don't know the man's name. "What's your name?"

"Killian. What's yours?" *Killy-in?* That's a funny name. Not so funny I want to laugh. But just kind of funny because I never heard that name before.

"Harmony. My real momma named me Harmony Carolina. But she left when I was a tiny baby." The man looks and feels sad. I can feel his sadness and it almost makes me sad too.

"Do you like ducks, Killy-in?"

It takes him a really long time to answer me. I hope he's not really afraid of ducks. These ducks are friendly ones. "Ducks? I can't remember ever having a feeling about ducks one way or the other."

I guess he's not ever seen a duck before. Poor Killy-in, the man with a funny name who's scared of me and never seen a duck before.

"I love the ducks. I love most all animals, except lions and bears, oh and sharks too. You know why? Because they eat people!" I hope there aren't any bears here. I never thought about it before. I grab Killy-in's hand just in case and squeeze it tight.

"Do you think bears or lions live in the woods around here?" I look across the big field and at the area with the trees at the end of the park.

"Well, I'm not from here, but I think we're safe." I think we're safe too. Miss Shelly would never take me to a park with bears. *Silly Harm.*

"Here Killy-in." I give him a crust from the bag and he takes it but just looks at it and then at me. He really is afraid of ducks. Maybe he's not seen them before.

"You do it like this." I pull my bread apart into tiny duck-sized pieces and throw it at them. The ducks start making their quacks and coming closer and closer. Killy-in looks both scared and mad at the ducks and I can't help it. I laugh so hard. When I do this Killy-in smiles a small smile. He's not afraid of the ducks any more. "They love crusts! You feed them too, Killy-in!"

We feed the ducks for a while, just listening to their happy quacks. Now that I am close to Killy-in I can see his tattoos on his arm better. It's like a pattern with things in it. One even looks like a stuffed animal. He's got the most tattoos I ever seen.

"You got lots of tattoos." I watch Killy-in but still face the ducks. I don't want to embarrass him because of his arms.

"I do. Do they bother you?" He holds out his arm for me, so I can look at them even closer. Yep that is definitely a stuffed animal- I think it's a dog. And there is a guitar. And some letters.

"Nope. They look like a coloring book. Some of them have a little color but the rest are waiting for more colors. This one is a purple seven." She points to one of seven sevens worked into my sleeve and chest piece. "Is seven your favorite number?"

He nods his head slowly "It is. Do you have a favorite number?"

Nobody ever asked me if I had a favorite number before. I'm not sure. I don't want to take Killy-in's favorite number. "I think nine is the best number. But seven is my second favorite!" I hope Killy likes the number 9 and it's not his most hated number or something. Then he might not want to be my friend.

"Do you live here Killy-in, by the park?" I give the ducks more of my bread.

"No. I live in Los Angeles, it's in California." Killy kicks a rock as he tells me about California. I give him more bread because he's out.

"Is that far away?" I ask him but I'm pretty sure it's far away.

"We took a plane to get here." Wow, I've never been on a plane before, that's amazing that he gets to fly up there in the top of the sky.

But he said we and I only see one man. "Who is we?"

"My fiancée. My brother and his wife. Our friend James. We all came together on the plane."

"I've never been on a plane before. Maybe one day I can fly somewhere too." I look at all the ducks. They never go on planes but they can fly, probably all the way to California if they wanted to. But I just stay here with Miss Shelly.

"Where would you fly to?" Killy asks me and then watches me really close, while I think where I would go if I could fly.

"To Disneyland. Or maybe the ocean so I can look for a real mermaid. I've never seen the real ocean before." I smile at him because I would love to see the ocean. I think California has one.

"Do you think mermaids are real, Killy-in? Miss Shelly says no, but I think so." I watch his reaction. Most boys laugh at me when I tell them I think mermaids are real. But Killy doesn't laugh at me. He thinks about it hard before he answers me.

"I've never seen one. But I've also never seen a real lion out in the jungle but they exist. I think it's possible mermaids are real." He's right! Just because we haven't seen them doesn't mean they aren't real. I knewed it! Mermaids are real!

"Here, your ducks are hungry." We are almost out of bread but I give Killy half of what is left because he's my new best friend besides Miss Shelly and Miss Banterworth and Ericka'in the back of the class.

"You're my new best friend Killy-in." I smile my biggest smile at him. "I really like you."

"Um, I like you too." He sounds nervous when he says it and I get that scared feeling from him again. It's like he's not sure he can believe that I like him. But of course I like him. He was brave feeding the ducks. And he thinks maybe mermaids are real and Miss Shelly doesn't even think that. Now instead of feeling scared he's feel love for me. It makes me all warm in a way I haven't felt before. I think Killy-in might be my real daddy. Miss Shelly told me he was out there and that one day he might even look for me because he didn't know I was real. But I am real. And I think that Killy is starting to love me back.

"I know you do. I feel it, right here." I touch my heart and Killy stops and looks at me with all of his heart. He is surprised I feel this. I wonder if he can feel me the same way. It's a weird thing.

"You feel me?" He looks at me, his mouth open just a little. Like he is surprised.

I nod "Yeah. It's weird. I never felt that before, it's almost like I know how your heart feels. I think it means we are supposed to be best friends. Let's walk around the path. It goes ALL the ways around the pond. Is that okay?"

"It's fine with me." He looks at the pond and I wonder if it looks as big to him as it does to me.

I grab Killy's hand and hold it tight. He has the best hands and my hand fits with his just right. I take him down the path that goes all the way around the pond. Killy doesn't say much so I start to tell him about my favorite Doc McStuffins. It's my favoritest cartoon. I don't think he's really listening to me though because he feels confused about me.

"Did you ever see that cartoon?" I ask him again even know I know that he probably didn't even hear what I was saying. "Killy-in? Did you see that one?"

"Um no. Sorry, I don't know that one. What else you like to do?" He looks at me like he's really paying attention to me now.

"I like to draw and color. My teacher says I'm a good artist. One time she even put my picture right in the middle of the bulleted board. I especially like when we sing in the morning. I'm even getting better at reading! I like stickers and unicorns and bright pink is my favorite color. Not the pale one but the really bright one! Oh, and sometimes I play mermaid in the bathtub." I look at Killy to see if he is going to laugh at me but he doesn't. Killy makes me feel safe when I want to tell him things. So I take a deep breath and tell him my secret.

"Sometimes I pretend my real mom was a mermaid. But that's just pretend. I don't think she's *really* a mermaid. But it makes me happier when I think she *is* a mermaid." I don't like to talk about my real mom much because it makes me sad that she never got better and came and got me.

"Killy-in? Do you know my foster mom?"

I shake my head. "No, I haven't met her yet."

"She's nice. Her name is Shelly. But she's not my real mom. That's what foster means. Shelly said my real mom's name is Sarah. Do you know my real mom?" I look up at Killy and it's almost like he's stopped breathing or is holding his breath at the pool. I think he might know my mom.

"Do you know her?" He doesn't say anything and just looks at me for a really long time. So long I think he might have forgotten I asked him a question. But then he nods his head very slowly and then squats so he can look me in the eye.

"I did know her, yes. I did know your real mom. She was my,

um, friend a long time ago." His eyes are waterlogged like he might cry any minute because he is sad for my mom. And that's when I know that Miss Shelly was right. My mom didn't come back for me because she died. And Killy is sad about that and sad for me too. I can feel Killy's sadness so deep in my heart it hurts me all the way to my bones. Poor Killy doesn't understand about how much my real mom loved me.

"She loved me so much. Miss Shelly told me that she loved me so much she found Miss Shelly to take care of me before I was even born. That's a lot of love huh Killy-in?"

"Yeah that is a lot of love." His voice is quiet like a mouse. I can barely hear it.

"I think she loved you too. My real mom." I wrap my arms around myself because Miss Shelly isn't here to hug me, and I don't think Killy is ready to hug me yet because he's still sad. "She was so sick and left me when I was real small with Miss Shelly. I wonder if my mom is still sick. Do you know Killy-in?"

Killy turns the whitest I ever seen a person be.

"Um." He doesn't say it, but I know I was right and it means my real mommy died and he already knowed that.

My real mom being dead makes Killy-in so sad. It makes me so sad too, but it makes Killy the most sad of all. He looks like he might cry and he's a grownup. I know he's not ready for this hug but I have to give it to him. His heart needs it and mine does too.

"It's okay, Killy-in." I grab him around the neck and hug him all the way to his bones because I don't want him to be so sad anymore. "It's okay." I pet his head like Miss Shelly does mine when I'm crying.

"Miss Shelly told me that she might be dead and I think, Killy-in, I already knowed she was. Or she would have come back for me. Right?" He kind of nods but it's hard for him because I'm still holding his head and petting it like a cat or maybe a dog, but Killy seems to like it so I do it more. I sniffle a

207

little bit because Killy-in's sad is reminding me how sad I get when I think about my real mom and how I was so tiny when she left I can't even remember her.

"Miss Shelly also says that one day my Daddy will come for me." I get this feeling from Killy, this idea like he might be my real Daddy and he's finally come for me. But when I said that he got all stiff and stopped breathing again.

"Killy-in?"

"Huh? What?" Killy-in gets all white again.

I'm so scared to tell him what I really think. What if he laughs at me and calls me stupid like Simon did at school when I told him mermaids were real. But my heart doesn't want to give up the chance to have a real Daddy. And I have to know if my heart is right. Because my heart feels like Killy is my real Dad.

"Are you my real daddy? I think maybe you might be because we have the same color eyes." I noticed it right when I saw him still holding my SamBear with the purple ribbon. His eyes are the same color blue as mine. And I've not seen anyone else but me with eyes this dark blue. Killy-in doesn't say anything, though.

"Are you here for me? Are you testing me to make sure I'm good? Because I am." I have to tell him how good I am, so he'll know and want to know me more and be my real Daddy. I don't think he's decided I'm good enough, so I have to tell him all the things I am good at. "I'm so good, Killy-in. I am. Ask anyone. Ask my Miss Shelly or Miss Drea. Or my teacher Miss Banterworth." He doesn't believe me. I can tell by his face, and I feel in my heart he's pulling away. But my teacher would tell him how good I'm doing in school. "Ask her! I'm getting better with my reading and I'm already real good with math. And I like to sing and draw. Are you here to take me home with you, Killy-in?"

He doesn't say anything but instead he stands up so I can't hug his neck anymore and he steps back and all I feel is that he's scared of me still...actually he's scared of me even more now than he was before. He steps back and runs his hand with the tattoos through his hair.

"I, um," he doesn't say any more words, but he doesn't have to. I get the picture now. Killy is my real Dad and he knowed it before he even came here. But he's too scared of me and doesn't want to know me. Maybe I'm not even good enough for him yet. I can't even get the words I want to say out. That I love him already because my heart knows him and that I'll do even more extra homework and get so good at reading. I take a deep breath because I know. Killy doesn't want to know me. I didn't pass his test. And it was my most important test I ever took.

"It's okay. I like Miss Shelly anyway." I turn away from in and back to the path we're standing in the middle of. "She says I can stay with her forever. We should finish our lap so I can go back to Miss Shelly. She misses me."

I start walking fast as I can walk on the path. I peek and Killy-in is walking behind me but he looks sad and he doesn't try to catch up even.

Well, too bad for him. I don't need Killy-in. I got Miss Shelly and she loves me even if I think mermaids are real. Even when I hide in the linen closet because there is too much noise or too much light, she still loves me and leaves me a snack and a flashlight in case it gets too dark in there.

He's probably wrong about my real Mom anyway. She's probably alive and a mermaid swimming in the Pacific ocean or maybe even the Indian ocean. I learned all about the different oceans on the Discovery channel.

When I finally get to the picnic area I march all the way to the table and pack crayons Drea brought for me. I crumple up my stupid picture of the stupid pond and the stupid ducks and throw it in the trash can. "I'm ready to go home Drea."

"It was nice to meet you Killian," Drea says. "Wasn't it, Harmony." She gives me that look that all grownups give me when they want me to agree with them. But I don't think it was nice to meet Killy-in because I didn't pass his test.

"Yeah sure. Bye." I turn back to the crayons to make sure I didn't miss any.

Drea says something else to Killy-in but I don't listen anymore. He's going to go to California or wherever he's from and forget about me. But that's okay because I got Miss Shelly.

"Want to go get an ice cream with me?" Drea holds out her hand to me. I don't really want an ice cream. I want Miss Shelly. But I know she has a meeting and Drea has to keep me longer, so I nod and watch Killy-in walk away to his big car, so he can fly away.

Chapter 39

The V (Sammy's POV)

Slipping into bed after a long night in the studio, I snuggle into Mel who's sleeping on her side, hugging her pregnancy pillow, her back to my front. Wrapping my arm around her, I lightly rub her rounded stomach. Seven and a half months into baking baby number five, Mel is insisting on me getting a vasectomy. She made the appointment, so I couldn't keep "forgetting" like I did after Axl was conceived.

We certainly weren't planning or even trying to get pregnant. But this baby, like brother Axl, is another seven percent baby. Mel's body just doesn't take well to the oral birth control pill, despite taking it daily.

Am I looking forward to having my balls snipped? No fucking way. But I'll do it for my girl. I'd do anything for my girl.

I rub my nose into the nap of her neck as she lets out a little snore. A side effect of pregnancy for her. I find it adorable, but learned with Allegra not to point it out, especially in front of others. She didn't talk to me for three days.

This baby is our second girl. We don't know for sure, but I've correctly guessed the sex of each of our four children and

I'm positive that number five is another girl. I've picked out the perfect name for her. Just like with the others we chose not to find out anything more than if it was healthy.

Mel says she doesn't care as long as it's a healthy baby. But I know she secretly wants another girl. We've been blessed to have healthy babies, and not counting the traumatic birth of Seven, run of the mill pregnancies and births.

I rub Mel's stomach again and feel my newest girl wiggle under my fingertips. Pregnancy is so fucking amazing, and Mel does it well. Another rub and more wiggles push against my fingertips. I can't wait to meet this little one, she's so sassy.

Mel flips my hand from her stomach. "Stop Sampson. I can't sleep with this baby rolling around on my spleen. Plus, you're making me hot." She scoots away from me slightly, and moans when I snuggle back up to her.

"Hmm you make me fucking hot Mel," I whisper, running my hand down her stomach to her core. The heat already emanates from her. "Fuck Mel, you're so sexy." I plant a kiss behind her ear as I grip her hip and pull her against me.

"You better follow through Sampson, if you're waking me up in the middle of the night." She pushes into my hand so reactive to me, but I have to be careful.

Another thing about my Mel and pregnancy? She's insatiable and sensitive. I can make her come with a few light touches. And have, many times. Most recently in Mav's driveway as she dropped me off for our writing and recording session in his studio.

"When have I ever failed to follow through? Ever?" I growl in her ear before nibbling on her neck and moving a hand to palm her full breasts. God this woman is sexy.

"Less talk. More action." She pushes back against me, and yelps with surprise when I roll onto my back bringing her with me. I'm sitting up and she's now in the crook between me and my bent knees, her round stomach grazing my abs.

She scrambles to lift herself and we watch together I guide her down on me. Her throaty moan turning me on even more as she envelops me completely.

"Oh, Sam. So good," She moans. The only time she calls me Sam is in the heat of passion.

"Shhh, babe. Don't wake Ax. Then I won't be able to follow through."

She throws her head back, that long dark hair that I love whipping my legs as she grounds herself into my pelvis. Steadying herself by gripping my shoulders, she squeezes tight as she takes over. I rest my hands on the round of her ass and squeeze, pulling her closer to me. Fuck she has a great ass. Surfing keeps it the perfect amount of firm and soft.

"Sam!" She half groans half shouts when I lean in and take a sensitive nipple into my mouth. I mean they are right there teasing me and I won't be able to enjoy them as she nurses our baby. I'll never get enough of this woman.

I knead her ass as she thrusts her pelvis forward and back faster, her breathing coming in short pants.

Her nails dig into my shoulders as she tightens around my cock.

She tenses her legs and her feet arc with her orgasm and I follow right behind her. "Fuck Mel."

We say in this position, forehead to forehead, while our heart rates slow. "I love you so much." I gently caress her hard stomach between us.

"I love you too Sampson. For reals." She leans forward and plants a kiss on my nose as she swings her leg over and waddles off to the bathroom.

"But you're still getting snipped today." She smirts over her shoulder at me as she settles back onto her side and I settle back in behind her.

R

"DADDY? YOU WAKED UP YET?" Axl, our youngest child, whispers from the far side of the bed. I've been awake for a bit, but I pretend to sleep because I love this game of ours and soon he'll be too big to play it.

"Daddy? You still seeping?" He says again, a little louder. Sheets tugs beneath me as he scales his mom's side of the bed. I release a loud breath for effect. Soon I feel his chubby fingers touch my nose and then poke in my ear.

"Daddy! Momma saided wake up time!" He pulls my eyelids apart, his own blue eye an inch from mine.

"She did?" I grab him around the middle and tickle his ribs, his blonde curls bouncing as he throws his head back in laughter.

"Stop Daddy! Ahh- I peeing! I peeing!" And sure enough, his wetness gets soaked up into my shirt and our bed sheets. Shit. Mel's gonna have a cow about that. I rise, pulling my shirt off and get to removing the sheets from our bed.

"Where's your diaper?" It's now I notice he's wearing only a t-shirt. No overnight pull-up. No underwear.

"I big boy wike you now."

"I don't pee the bed. And I don't walk around without pants on."

"But you ticklin' me!" He sticks his bottom lip out and looks at me through his long brown eyelashes. I can't resist this kid. He may have been a surprise, but he's the best kind of surprise, just like the new baby will be.

My second oldest son, Lud, bounds into the room. "Mom says it's breakfast time. Where's Ax's pull-up?"

"That's the question." I mumble as I wad up the soiled sheets and toss them into the laundry basket.

"Mom said to tell you that you're not getting out of the snip-snip today and to get dressed. Uncle Kill will be here soon."

"What's the snip-snip daddy?" Allegra joins us, hugging her stuffed Lion toy. "Can I get a snip-snip with you too?"

"No- that's only for old dudes," Seven, my first born, responds as he swoops Axl up. "Let's get some pants on little man. Before Killian comes over and sees your penis out and about."

"Seven! Don't encourage him." I admonish without really meaning it. I'm sure Killian wouldn't be phased in the least to find a naked from the waist down toddler roaming my house.

"Peenee out and about!" Axl screeches in hysterical laughter. "Kiwi not seein' my peenee! It pivate!"

"It's not private if you don't have pants on." Seven carries his little brother out of the room, Axl's laugh carrying all the way down the hall.

"So, I can come get a snip-snip with you and Uncle Kiwi? Please Daddy?"

"No. Sorry hon. It's nothing exciting, I promise." I pull a new shirt on. Thank God I put my shorts on after I went to the bathroom. "Let's go see what mom made for breakfast."

"Cereal." She rolls her eyes with exasperation. She's her mom in all the best ways, especially with the eye rolling. "Again."

"There's nothing wrong with cereal. I love cereal."

"Not the good kinds." She huffs as we head towards the kitchen.

Allegra wasn't lying. Mel has everyone's bowl of Rice Krispies ready, complete with a side of sliced bananas and apples. So much so that they are soggy by the time I get to mine.

"Killian will be here in fifteen." Mel leans in and kisses my forehead as I shovel my now silent cereal mush into my mouth and encourage the kids to do it as well.

"Why can't you take me again?" I glance up at her as she skins Allegra's apple slices for her. Allegra is a diva through and through. No crusts, no skins, and nothing green should pass her lips.

"Because either Kill takes you, or I take you and Kill stays with the kids. I don't want to come home to him locked in the pantry again. He's too gullible." I chuckle with Mel.

That was funny. Killian was not amused but had only been locked in for about ten minutes before we got home. It's not like Seven wasn't here to watch the brood. Or that Killian'd go hungry. The pantry is literally where all the best snacks are and he's tall enough to reach them without scaling the shelves ala Axl.

True to his word, Killian, donning his typical black t-shirt black jeans ensemble, strolls into the house.

"Uncle Kiwi!" Allegra and Axl shriek in unison as they throw themselves at him.

"Look! Pants!" Ax pulls at the band of his sweatpants. "No peenee out!" He grins at his uncle, my best friend. Ax knows no enemies. He's a lover of everyone.

Killian chuckles at my youngest. "That's good, bud. You should keep that under wraps." He tousles Ax's hair then arches a brow at me with a smile. I just shrug.

Allegra tugs his shirt as I shove the last bit of banana in my mouth. "Kiwi, can I come to get a haircut too?" I love that my kids all call him Kiwi. It was started by Gibson, who made sure to teach all of his cousins, blood and band, that Killian was to be called Uncle Kiwi or Kiwi for short.

Killian looks at my daughter perplexed. "Haircut?" He tips his head to the left as he tries to figure out what Allegra is asking him. I don't know if Killian even realizes Allegra has a huge crush on him. She's all about Uncle Kiwi. If he's over, she's chatting with him, doing her everything to try to get his attention.

"The snip-snip?" She looks up at him with her big doe eyes full of innocence and motions scissors with her hand.

His deep hearty laugh makes us all laugh, even Allegra for whom Kill can do no wrong. She has no idea why this is so funny, which makes it even funnier.

"Honey, they are going to a doctor appointment not a hair appointment," Mel explains, coming to Killian's aid.

"Oh."

"Speaking of which, Sammy, we better roll." Killian slaps me on the back and we move out to his SUV in the driveway. We drive quietly for a few minutes.

"You really doing this?" He gives me side eye as he drives us out of my neighborhood.

"Yeah." He knows I promised Mel after Ax too. "Mel made the appointment and everything. She's done with the pregnancy part of parenthood. It's a lot to be pregnant I think." He nods quietly as he turns onto the freeway.

I worry briefly about my friend. Where Mel and I have been blessed with easy fertility, it's been a struggle for Killian and Vi. They got pregnant with Fender soon after Harmony came to live with them. They tried for one more. Vi got pregnant a few times but miscarried each time. The last time was especially hard on Vi physically and on both of them emotionally. They since stopped trying.

"It's easier on Mel if I get it taken care of instead of her having her tubes tied or whatever." I shrug.

"You realize they're going to punch a hole in your ball sack, right? Then they'll pull out your sperm tubes like spaghetti noodles and cut and cauterize them and stuff em back in. I read all about how they do it. They call it the scalpel-less surgery."

"Did you have to ruin spaghetti for me?"

He shrugs as he pulls into the doctor's office parking lot. "Just preparing you. Did you shave yourself? Even if you did, they may shave you anyway- if you didn't get it close enough or whatever. I read about that too. Who wants to have to shave another man's nutsack?"

"Well aren't you Mr. Education." I can't help my snark.

"I was thinking of having a vasectomy, but ultimately Vi decided on the tube thing. Part of the tubal thing was gaining control back over her fertility.

"I was willing to get the snip, but that last loss broke her, man. She was done." He grows quiet and I know he's remembering us cutting the tour short so he could go home. I don't know all the details, but I know he was worried about Vi. We all were.

R

"THEY LET me watch the whole thing!" I exclaim, relieved the deed is done. Killian's quiet again as we wait for the lady to make my follow up appointment, where they test my spunk to make sure I'm shooting blanks or whatever.

"It was kind of cool." I repeat to Killian as we buckle our belts. "I couldn't feel a damn thing. Just call me captain dead balls."

He shakes his head and slips his phone into the cubby of his center console as he drives me home.

As we pull back into Casa Denton, it looks like the gang's all here.

"Are we writing or having a party?" I look at Killian. "I'm supposed to stay off my feet for a few days. I'm not sure why- it's not like I walk on my balls."

Killian about spits out the swig of water he just took from his bottle. "You better quit with all the ball talk. There are kids running around."

"I can't not talk about my balls. They're numb as fuck. It's truly weird."

He slaps my back and I meander into the house, where the

kids have decorated a chair with balloons and stickers. Mav stands behind the chair.

"Come on, DB, sit in your thrown." He motions to the decked out chair.

"DB?" I look at Mav.

"Dead balls." Seven barks out from across the room.

"Seven!" His mom yells at him. "Language."

"What am I supposed to call them, Mom? Nuts? Cajones? Nads?" He looks at his mom, knowing he's pushing her buttons. On purpose.

"Let's not talk about them at all." She says handing me a special ice pack.

"I got to watch the whole thing." I exclaim and then proceed to tell the story to the guys as the women and children go play in the pool.

"Dude, are you gonna pass out?" Callum looks absolutely ashen when I talk about how they put the hole in my balls and then reached in with these tiny micro grabber things.

Killian walks in from outside and wordlessly grabs his brother by the elbow and guides him over to the couch. "Sit before you pass out and get a concussion, again."

Chapter 40

The Last Angel (POVs: Killian, Harmony, Vi)

"How is she?" I whisper, quietly shutting the hospital door behind me. "I got here as soon as I could."

"I know you did," Arista says with a hoarse whisper, her eyes shiny with fresh tears as she reaches out to grab my arm. "She'll be okay." She sighs as if the world is on her shoulders.

"It was bad Kill, after, um she lost some blood so she's a little weak. She's devastated, understandably. She wouldn't stop crying. They had to give her a sedative, so she'd rest. She's out now." Ari's chin quivers and she glances over to Vi.

My heart drops to my feet when I get my first look at my ocean princess, my real life mermaid, as she lays in the hospital bed. She's so pale it makes her hair look even darker, despite the fact that she'd stopped dying it so it's faded and grown out from the dark brown she'd been sporting. An IV in the arm closest to me, still drips fluid into her. Her head faces the side away from me.

And what's worse? She still looks pregnant. I can't help but stare at the sheet pulled tight around her little rounded abdomen. She'd just started showing a week before I left. And now it's empty. Just like I am. It's an utter devastation I don't know how we'll get through.

I fucking knew better than to go. I didn't want to leave on this sixteen-day tour of the east coast. "It's barely over two weeks." Mav urged. The band knew I didn't want to leave Vi, that she couldn't and shouldn't come with us either. "We need you Kill."

Well so did my wife. I'll never forgive him. Them. My hands ball up so tight in a pent-up rage, that my nails dig into the palms of my hand. I haven't felt rage like this before. I've never been a fighter. So sure we were in the clear, I agreed on the tour.

And now that's something I can't get back. I wasn't here to support her. To hold her. To say goodbye to our baby. Our third angel.

She was well into her second trimester. Our previous two pregnancies after Fender were lost at nine and seven weeks respectively. We lost this one at seventeen weeks. *Seventeen.*

Would it have been any easier to have been here with her? Absolutely not. But I would have fucking been here with my wife and not across the country in Bumfuck, Maine, while she lost our child. I'm beyond sad, right now I'm fucking seething.

Ari's hand brushes my arm and pulls me out of my head. "I don't want to worry you anymore Kill, but Harmony's aware of what's happened. Mel says she's upset and scared but she's been talking to her about it."

I can't be more grateful for the wives of my bandmates. Especially Mel and Ari. Mel's the perfect person to help Harmony understand what's happened. And being around her cousins is probably good for her right now.

"Fend?" I ask after my toddler.

"He's fine. He's too young to understand anything." She tries to reassure me but I'm not so sure. Fender's not your typical three-year-old, if my bandmate's kids are anything to compare him to. He's quiet, thoughtful, and surprisingly empathetic. He knows when someone in his world is suffering and no doubt he knows something's up, I'd bet my money on it. He's also incredibly in-tune to his mom, and she to he.

"I should have been here." I mutter.

"There was no way you could have known Killian. No one would have guessed this one." Ari squeezes my arm but I barely feel it as my eyes return to my wife in her hospital bed. "I'm going to go pick up Harm and Fend and take them home with me. Is that okay?"

I nod. They need me, but so does my wife.

"Try to rest. She'll need you when she wakes up. The kids will be fine with me." Ari leaves me with my wife.

I pull the chair close to Vi's bed, but push her hair from her forehead and kiss it before I settle with her hand in mine in the chair. "I'm here beautiful."

"I'm so so sorry I wasn't here with you. Forgive me." I sob quietly, finally letting the loss out, while no one can witness my breakdown. My phone vibrates in my back pocket. I check to make sure that it's not Ari or Mel and when I see it's my brother I throw it against the wall opposite of the bed. *Too fucking late, asshole. Too fucking late.*

The noise has nurses running into the room, fearful that Vi's fallen out of bed.

"Sorry. It was me. Sorry." I lift my arms in apology and retrieve my now cracked and probably destroyed phone.

Our obstetrician comes in to talk with me when she finds out I'm here. "You couldn't have prevented this Killian. She knows that." Her words are meant to give me solace, but they spark another wave of white hot anger in me instead. "Sometimes these things just happen for no discernible reason. And it's not fair." So much so that I hold it in instead of unleashing the vitriol in my heart and head onto the unsuspecting doctor.

I could have supported her. How Vi will ever forgive me, for not being here with her? How will I forgive me? I return to my wife's bedside, holding vigil over her until she wakes.

R

"Dad?" I look up from my guitar and Harmony's got Fender on her hip, carrying him just like Vi does, looking like a mom. If that's not a mind fuck. My baby girl being a mom? Not going there any time soon. Her forehead's wrinkled, so I set my guitar in its stand.

"What's up, Harm?"

"Momma cwyin." Fender's face crumples and tears pour down his despondent little face. "Momma so sad." Yeah, I know buddy. It hurts my heart too, buddy. I'm not sure if I should console Fender or go check on Vi.

"Check Mom. I got him." Harmony pulls her brother closer to her, nuzzling into him and whispering something that calms him. She's such a good sister to him.

Vi's been chilly towards me since we came home from the hospital over a week ago. First, she demanded that I go back and finish the tour, which I told her like fucking hell. She won't let me hold her. She won't talk to me. She won't rage at me like I deserve. It's like I'm not here.

She barely leaves the bed, let alone the bedroom, so I don't have to search for her. Sure enough when I open the bedroom door, she's curled up in a fetal position sobbing big, racking sobs. Her hands are fisted, scrunching up the sheet in angry balls in each one.

I slip into a sitting position on the bed and wrap my arms around her. Pulling her up to rest on my chest, I don't tell her not to cry or try to shush her. I just hold her to me and gently caress her arm. I tell her I love her. That I'm sorry I wasn't there. That I'll always love her. Anything that comes to mind, even though it's not enough.

I don't know how long we're like this on our bed. Her breathing eventually evens out and I hold her as she sleeps. Still holding her, I manage to dislodge my still busted up phone from my pocket and text Ari.

> Me: Can you come and pick up the kids. Get dinner with them or something?

> Ari: Of course. I'll keep them for the night if you want.

> Me: That'd be great.

> Ari: I'll be by in 15.

> Ari: How is she?

> Me: Not good, but at least she's letting me hold her today. Thanks for doing this for me. I'll make sure they're ready.

> Me to Harmony: Ari's coming to get you both for a sleepover. Can you pack a bag for you both? Make sure to take Fend's blanket and have him pick a buddy. Take extra pull-ups just in case.

> Harm: Okay. Is mom okay?

Well shit. How do I answer that? I want to reassure my daughter. But there is nothing okay about either of us right now.

> Me: She's really sad about the baby. We both are. We'll talk tomorrow okay?

> Harm: Kay. Love you.

> Me: I love you too.

I hear Harmony quietly collect things for their sleepover with Ari and Gibson and their girls. The band comes home tomorrow. I know Callum'll try to come over. I hope Ari tells him to butt the fuck out. I really don't think I can look any of them in the face right now.

It's dark by the time Vi stirs and without kids the house is uncharacteristically quiet.

"Harm!" She calls out loudly, looking startled. "Fend?!" Her hair's a mess and she's on day three of the same sweatpants and t-shirt. But she's still my beautiful girl.

"They're at a sleepover with Gibs, Tay and Daiz."

"Oh. I didn't know."

"Ari offered and I didn't want to wake you. They're worried about you."

"The kids?"

I nod, wanting to keep their worries off of her, knowing that the information will crush her. But I can't so I squeeze her to me and explain in hushed tones. "You know how perceptive Fend is especially when it comes to you. And Harm looks up to you so much. She's been helpful with Fend. She emulates things you do to try to help him and me. But she's just a girl and she's scared and sad too." Vi takes a huge shuddering breath and I rub her back before I continue, still holding her to me.

"We all are worried about you. This isn't like you, Vi. I'm not saying it's not soul crushing, and I know you're mad at me for not being here. Hell, I'm fucking furious with the band, our manager, the label, but mostly with myself. But right now, my focus is on you. How I can help you? Can I help you? Is me being here really too hard?"

My quiet questions hang in the air around us. I don't even know if I expect her to answer. Or if she's capable of answering. She's so broken and *I* contributed to that. And that's what fucking slays me right now. She might never be able to forgive me, from that.

225

She shudders with sobs as I rock her. "I just...I dunno. I'm flummoxed babe. I understand the grief. I feel it deep in my bones too." I stop, catching my own tortured sob before it escapes and makes everything worse. "I know I can't fix this. That there isn't a fix for it. But I'm scared. You hiding in the bedroom all day, it's not healthy. You're not eating enough. The kids really miss you and don't understand. I miss you. Your sister's worried."

At the mention of Ari, my phone vibrates against the stand nightstand. I check it just to make sure, it's not her. It's Callum. Again.

Vi looks up at me with a question on her face, and a crease in her brow as I unwrap my arms from around her. She's worried it's about the kids, too. Hating to disengage from that contact I so needed, she sits up and puts a hand on my thigh.

Fuck you Callum! I scream it in my head and not out loud like I want to. She startles when I pitch my phone across the room for the third time this week. This time it crashes into the sliding door to our master balcony. Vi worked hard to make the balcony our special place, where we hold each other and relax in the evening. The French door spider webs like it was hit with a baseball and my phone hits the floor. Again. It's got to be dead this time.

Vi looks back and forth between the phone and me, her brows pulled together. She squeezes my thigh. Her voice is soft when she repeats my words back to me. "How can *I* help you? *Can* I help you?"

"I guess you could say I'm firmly in the anger stage." I attempt to shrug off my behavior and turn my back to her as we sit on our bed. How dare I show my pain, my grief when hers is so much worse. My jaw tightens as my teeth clench so hard I'm worried I'll break a tooth.

I put my hands on my thighs, about to get up to retrieve my phone when I feel something unexpected. She gives my shoulder gives a slight squeeze and I drop my chin to my chest. I don't deserve this kindness from her. I deserve all her rage and ire for not being here.

"Kill..." her voice trails off and her hand drops off me when I stand abruptly to get my phone. I don't deserve her comfort.

"I..." I head towards our bedroom door. "I gotta get a new phone." My need to get away from here sudden and necessary. Before I say something I shouldn't.

"Killian, it's late. We can do it tomorrow." Her voice trails off behind me as I head straight through the house into the garage and uncover the Maybach. I haven't driven her lately, so she needs a running. I was considering trading her in for an SUV similar to the one Vi has, but this car has so much sentimental value to me. I don't know if I can.

I'm about a mile away, when I realize she said we. *"We can do it tomorrow."* Shit. I fucked up again. She was reaching out. Connecting. Trying to come back to us and I just left.

I probably should have turned around. But I didn't.

ᚱ

IT'S EVEN LATER when I get home, forgetting how much time it takes to get a new phone. Why does it take so damn long?

I expect the house to be dark, but it's not. It looks like it used to. Like the dark cloud that has been over it the last eleven days has moved on. Moana is playing on the television and the Vi, who looks like she's taken a shower and dressed is flanked by each kid.

"You're back." Vi says and Fender frowns.

"Boken o' all betta?" He throws his hands up wondering about my phone.

"I got a new one buddy. This one's all better." I pull my phone out of my hoodie pocket so he can see it.

"There's still popcorn daddy." Our beautiful daughter motions to the bowl on her lap.

"Still bobcorn daddy." Fender parrots his sister.

"Sit with us babe." My wife say. "Watch Moana."

"Netfix! And seals!" Fender giggles.

"Wait did he just..."

Vi nods. "Yes. You can thank Mav for that one."

"Mav?" When?

She nods and shoots me a 'we'll talk later' look.

I slip under our giant movie blanket next to Harmony, who sets the half-full popcorn bowl on my lap once I'm settled in. Fender passes out across Vi's lap, his head on Harmony's leg about a third of the way in. When the movie's over, I pick up my sack of potatoes son and carry him to bed. When I return to the living room, Harmony's hugging Vi.

"Night Daddy." She turns and hugs me before heading off to her bedroom.

"What happened to their sleepover with Ari and their kids?"

"I needed my kids." Vi pats the couch next to her and hooks her head towards the seat next to her and holds up the movie blanket. "Just like I need you."

I crawl under the blanket with my wife and she immediately snuggles up to me, laying her head on my heart, on her tattoo. For the first time since I returned home, I feel a slight peace as I wrap my arms around her.

"Kill?" I look down at her, as she looks up at me. Her big hazel eyes fill up with tears. "I'm sorry I checked out. That wasn't fair to you or the kids." She takes a deep breath, and a squeeze her a little to let her know it's okay to feel. I kiss her forehead. "You have every right to check out. I was just worried you weren't going to check back in." I rub her back.

She runs her fingers lightly over my chest as she snuggles back into me, tucking her head under my chin. Just being so close is such a salve to my soul. "You were right, the kids were both upset and scared." I nod against the top of her head. "Harmony wants to talk tomorrow."

"That's my fault. I told her I'd talk to her tomorrow. I wasn't expecting you..."

"To be a mom?" She says harshly of herself.

"I was going to say to turn around so quickly. You were so ensconced in the black cloud that I was worried I'd lose you to it. That..." I let my voice trail off because I don't want to put ideas in her head about removing me from her life. I don't want her to be so angry with me, and I worry that part is still coming.

"That what? Killian..." She pulls out of my grip to look me in straight in the eye.

"That we were broken. You have every reason to be angry with me...to hate me." *To leave me.* I can't say that. I don't dare put those words out into the universe.

She lays her palm to my cheek and I turn my face to kiss the heart of her hand.

"Killian...I love you."

"I love you too." I say automatically. Because I do. I always will.

"No. I *love* you." She stares into my eyes and I'm naked, despite being fully clothed. Only Vi can strip away everything, all the walls I still build despite not even realizing I'm doing it.

"I..." She puts two fingers against my lips.

"I know you and I know your heart, Killian Donogue." Her feather light kiss brushes my lips where her fingers were seconds ago. "It hurts my heart that you feel so unworthy of love. Still. After I promised not only to love you, but to take care of your heart for the rest of my life in our wedding vows. I didn't take those words lightly either time and I still don't now."

I blink rapidly trying to keep the tears at bay, remembering both of our weddings. Our small intimate one at the courthouse before Fender came and the one we had after he was born that was for our friends and family. Our vows were identical at both. *"I vow to love, cherish, and take care of your heart in sickness and in health, in good times and hard times, for as long as we both shall live."*

"I'm worried about you."

"About me?"

She nods slowly and strokes the side of my face. "You're anger. You mentioned you were incredibly angry at the band."

"I didn't want to leave you. They knew that. Look what happened when I did."

"Killian, this would have happened if you were here or not. It's not meant to be. We have the family we're meant to have."

"Still, I should have been here to support you, to hold you while, well, you know." She caresses my cheek softly again. It's distracting because it's a little more stubbly than I normally keep it, which is probably why she keeps running her hand over it. Her last spoken words are just now sticking to my brain. *"We have the family we're meant to have."* She wants to stop trying for another baby. Instantly I am both relieved and a little sad. I don't know how many more losses she can take. We can take.

"I'm good with that." I lock eyes with her because I need her to see I'm telling the truth. I'm not the one who does the hard work there and I know it. She leans in and kisses my nose.

"We'll talk about what that means later, okay?" She asks. I nod and lean in for another kiss, but she denies me.

"So Kady told me the band came back the next morning. They want to support you. Us. But you've been avoiding your brother for almost a week. She said he's reached out multiple times."

My jaw clenches without warning. Just hearing their names, just the idea of the band I use to love and now resent tenses my entire body. Vi notices.

"Now can we talk about all that anger you're harboring?"

Harmony, the next day

"Daddy?" He's been playing guitar and writing songs about his feelings. It's what my dad does. Especially when he's confused or overwelled, which is our word for overwhelmed. Most of his songs stay here in our house, but sometimes he takes them with him and makes them Blind Rebels songs.

"Hey Harm, I didn't hear you come in." He sets his guitar down and pats the couch next to him. "What's up, buttercup?" He smiles at me as he pushes his hair out of his eyes.

"Yesterday you said we'd talk, remember?" I pull the pillow onto my lap and run my hand back and forth on it watching the sequence change in pattern.

"Sure. So let's talk. Do you want mom too?" He asks me.

I shake my head.

"Are you sure?"

"She's trying to get Fender to take a nap. I wanted to talk to just you anyway."

"Okay. Well, Aunt Mel explained what was happening with mom and the baby right? " He looks like he's scared, like he needs to explain where babies come from. Mom and I had already been talking about that kind of thing.

"I know about babies and stuff. And Mel told me all about the baby and how it was way too early so it wouldn't be okay and stuff." I look at my shoes.

Dad doesn't say anything. He's waiting for me, like mom waits for him to talk sometimes so he can think first. I don't know how to ask what I want to ask without upsetting him. He rubs my shoulder.

"I did something because I was sad and you were worried about mom. And Mom was too sad to get out of bed. But now I'm worried Mom will get mad if she sees what I did." *And she'll make him take me back to Montana and Miss Shelly.* I am probably going to have to show it to him so he can decide.

Dad squeezes my shoulder and tilts his head.

"What did you do?" He asks, his head tilts to the side like when he's really curious.

"I was sad and looking at some of the baby stuff we had for him. I was so mad he wasn't coming any more. And sad I wouldn't have another brother. But also mad cuz everyone was so sad."

"Okay. It's okay to have big feels about this Harm. We all do. We're all mad and sad. I think even Fender is in his own way."

"But I did something and Vi's going to be so mad." Stupid tears come out of my eyes even though I don't want them to. I want to just get this over with and find out if they'll be too mad at me and send me back to Miss Shelly.

"What did you do?"

"I cut some of his clothes and stuff up. Like destroyed it. But then I was sorry I did it. So I made something out of it in the studio. But now that mom's feeling a little better, I'm worried she'll see it and get mad. Or really sad again." And send me back.

"Where did you say mom is?"

"Taking a nap with Fend in your bedroom."

Dad stands and reaches his hand out to me. "Show me, kiddo."

We walk out of the music room and to the studio room where my mom keeps all the painting stuff. We have other art stuff in there too but mom mostly paints and sometimes I paint with her. Sometimes we do other stuff. It's the creative place. We don't even have to be quiet because the bedrooms are on the other side of the house and we can watch Fend during his naps on Mom's phone.

We close the door and I go into the supply closet and pull out my creation. It's on one of mom's big canvases that I don't usually use but I felt like I needed extra space. It's what mom taught me is called mixed medium because I used more than just paint. I used paint and pieces of baby clothes and some of the baby toys that were easy to cut or pull apart.

I put it in my easel for Dad to look at, kind of like when Mom and me do art shows for him or the family for fun. We like showing what we are working on and hearing what they say. Good or bad mom says, it's a reaction and that's all you can ask for.

I step back and Dad steps closer. He doesn't say anything. He looks at it and then tips his head and looks at it some more. Then he gets closer and does the same thing again. My stomach does flip flops because I can't tell if he's mad or sad I ruined the baby things.

"I can use my 'llowance to buy the stuff I ruined." I whisper. "Please don't send me back."

I can't tell if he heard me because he just makes a noise and keeps looking at the canvas. But then he whips his head and looks at me.

"Wait what?" He looks at me. "What did you say Harm?"

"That I can use my 'llowance to buy the stuff I ruined?" My voice cracks.

"No, the other thing you said." He squats down. "The other thing you said hon. What was it?"

I gulp so big that air goes all the way down. Like I'm getting ready to try to make a big burp.

"Um, please don't send me back." It's so quiet in the house now, I worry Dad can hear my thoughts. He can sometimes. I don't want him to know that I still worry about them deciding they don't want me anymore.

"Back where?" His voice is quiet and calm, so I don't think he will. But sometimes I worry that it will happen when I least expect it.

"Back to Miss Shelly. Back to Montana."

"Oh Harm, baby." He pulls me in for a hug and squeezes me just the right amount. I love my dad's hugs. He gives the best

233

ones in the world. I use to think Miss Shelly's were the best, but nope. Dad's are.

"We would never send you back. You're our daughter. Our family. Sending you back would never ever happen." His eyes are wet like mine. It's like he's going to start crying.

"Harm, it's been over three years. Why would we send you back sweet girl?"

"I dunno. Sometimes, I worry about it." My words are shaky like I am going to cry too. "Like maybe you'll decide I'm too much or not enough. I always try to be just right."

He hugs me and rocks me. "We would never, ever send you back. For any reason. Okay?" I can't answer because now I'm crying. He pulls back so he can look at my face.

"Okay?" He looks right in my eyes, so I know he means it.

I just nod and don't say anything.

"I think we're going to have to talk about this again. Maybe with mom too? Not because you're in trouble but because I'm really sad you still worry about being sent back, sweet girl."

He whispers in my ear while giving me another perfect hug. "Never gonna happen, okay?"

"Kay."

"Now that's settled we need to talk about this mixed medium art you made." He moves us over to my canvas and touches the part in the middle. "You made this by yourself?"

"Yes. Mom didn't even know."

"Harm, I feel your feelings when I look at this. Your confusion and sadness and...anger. All of it. That's what art is supposed to do right? Make people feel something when they look at it." Dad looks at me. He knows music and Mom knows about art. I know a little about both.

"It's one of my favorite things you've ever made." He says it in his serious voice, that means he means it.

"We need to show this to your mom."

"But I ruined the baby's stuff to make it. I don't want to

234

make her mad. Or sad. I especially don't want to make her sad again."

"You're sad about the baby, right?" I nod at Dad's question. "But making this made you feel a little better right? Getting all the emotions out?"

"That's exactly right."

"That's how it feels for me to write a song. It's why I've been in the music room a lot. Seeing this makes me understand that is why you made this. You're making room for all the emotions inside, so they don't get all tangled up. Your mom will understand that too. We'll show her together after their nap."

Vi- After the nap

A chubby finger goes in my earhole. I don't know what is with this kid of mine and sticking his fingers into ears. Then I feel his slobbery mouth on my cheek in an open mouth kiss. "Momma? I waked up now."

"Me too buddy."

"I pee pee?" He shifts around on my bed and I jump up and swoop him off the sheets and into the ensuite bathroom and hold him on our toilet, the only bathroom in the house that doesn't have a toddler sized seat addition.

We make a big deal out of flushing and washing our hands.

"Hungwy! 'Nack time?" He gives me side eye.

"We'll see. It's close to dinner time."

He gives me side-eye with a pout this time. The faces this boy has at his disposal. I hug him to me and breath in his toddler scent. We are so lucky to have this one.

We come out and I start making a snack for Mr. Hungry-pants. "Kill? Harm? You want ants on a stick?"

Fender giggles at the name as I slather peanut butter into his celery sticks. This is his favorite snack and I think it's all about the name.

Kill and Harm come into the kitchen from the other side of the house.

My husband sits at the breakfast bar next to where Fender sits on his knees waiting for his ant sticks. "I'll have one."

"No thanks." Harmony replies, flopping onto the couch. She's not a huge fan of celery, but she'll eat them sometimes, so I always offer.

"When we're done here," Killian starts after eating the raisins off his celery stick. "Harm wants to show you something she made."

Now I am curious. If she wanted to show me something why didn't she just do it? I hope that Harmony doesn't resent me for checking out for a while. I know Killian's talked to her about it, but I think I need to as well. Apologize. She was worried about me and scared, and dealing with her own feelings of loss of the baby. Mother of the year right here.

"Ready?" Killian says to me as he scoops up Fender. I nod.

"Come on Harm." He hooks his head motioning to our daughter to follow while Fender shoves a finger in his ear.

We head down towards the art studio, likely why Killian has Fender. I've had him in there a few times, but he's like a tornado and messes it up.

In the studio, a big canvas sits on Harm's easel. There are wide strokes of different blues with some black and dark purple. There's an overall tone of melancholy in the colors and strokes. But there's also sadness, with a touch of anger on this canvas. Random pieces of plastic are glued on. But in the center is what looks like an angel made from glued fabric and plastic in the center of the canvas. Complete with a halo.

"You made this?" She nods at my question. "And Killian didn't help?"

"No. He didn't even know I was in here."

"Harmony. This. This is amazing."

"You're not mad? I used the baby's stuff." Harmony sniffles

as tears start to roll down her cheeks. I'm not sure if it's because she's sad for our loss or because she was that worried I'd be upset.

Harmony may not have come from my womb but she is my daughter all the same. Her art proves that. She used things we'd done messing around in the art studio, things we did for fun and to bond and used them to express her emotions at a time when she probably felt like she didn't have another way to express them. I am touched, I am proud. I love this girl more than life itself. She's a talented musician naturally and loves to sing and play around in the music room with her dad. But she's an immensely talented artist too.

"You only forgot one thing." I tell her.

"What did I forget?" She looks back at her canvas scanning it.

"You forgot the sign the corner. Remember?" She grabs a paint pen and makes her initials HD.

"Do you have a name for it?" I turn the canvas over and take the paint pen from her hand.

"The Last Angel."

Now it's my turn to have tears pouring down my face. The name couldn't be more perfect. I carefully write the name, the date and Harmony's full name on the backside of the canvas as is our tradition.

"Is it okay with you if I hang this one in our bedroom?" I hope she doesn't think that I want to hide it in there.

"You want to put it in your bedroom?" She repeats, looking at me like she's shocked. "Why?"

"I want it there, so I'll see it every day. To remember our last angel and to remember the two I have here with us."

Chapter 41

The Blind Rebel's Interview

This interview initially appeared on Carla Dufraine's Rock&Metal Roundup Interview with the Blind Rebels Blog.

I've had the pleasure of exclusive interviews with the Blind Rebels for many years and today's interview is no different. But the Blind Rebels that I'm interviewing today is quite a different band from back in the day when it wasn't uncommon for them to do the cliché rock n roll things like throwing furniture off the balcony of their hotel.

This is a more settled Blind Rebels. Two of the members even have children in tow today. But I am lucky to get all four members in the room with me today, just like back in the old days.

Thank you all for agreeing to sit with me and interview like we use to when you were first starting out. This new album, **Rock The World Revisited,** is a departure from your normal, gritty Rebels rock n' roll we are use to. Can you just talk a little about this new album for our readers?

Mav: Thanks Carla. This album is exactly what the title

insinuates. It revisits our most popular album Rock The World from five...

Cal: Seven. It was seven years ago, Mav.

Mav gives Callum a disbelieving look and makes a whistling sound before he corrects himself: Seven years ago. Some songs have been slowed down and turned into ballads. Others are done acoustically. Each song off the original album is reimagined in some manner. And we've added a second album of new music that we've written that we think follows the Rock The World album well.

Carla: Is there anything else different about this album that listeners would like to know?

Sammy: Yeah, we all wrote on this one. On a lot of our previous albums Mav and Callum did most of the writing, but this time Killian and I wrote some of the songs too. It's probably not a surprise, but Killian is quite the songwriter. Right Kill?

At this point, Killian, who's carrying an infant covered in a black blanket in a carrying pack looks up and shrugs.

Killian: I mean, I guess. Sometimes it's easier for me to express things through music. Most of those don't get brought to the band. But a few do.

Cal: Don't let his humility fool you, my brother is an amazing songwriter. He's got a talent I wish he had shared earlier in our journey as a band.

Killian: I mean I did...

Cal: I just wish you'd have been more...insistent Bubs.

Carla: Bubs?

Cal: Childhood familial nickname. You'll edit that part out, right?

Carla: Speaking of songwriting, what is your key inspiration? Is it purely your own life/experiences, or about other people?

Mav: I think it's different for each of us. When I'm writing it's usually something I've seen or heard. A lot of times, at least lately, it's based off something Kady has said to me.

Cal: For me it can be anything, from seeing Ari with or children, maybe something Gibson has said.

At his name Gibson looks up from the table where he's contently coloring, and tilts his head.

Gibson: You write songs about my words?

Cal chuckles before answering: Yep buddy sometimes.

Gibson: I write songs too!

Cal: Yeah, you do. Okay you finish your picture for Ari while we finish our interview okay?

Gibson returns to his drawing.

Sammy: For me it's primal- I don't do much songwriting to be honest. I've written or co-written a few here or there but for me it's always about the rhythm before anything. But for this album I wrote two songs.

Kill: Why are you all looking at me? I guess for me when I'm writing it usually comes from a place of emotion, like something I'm experiencing that I'm having trouble putting into actual words. I use the music to say it for me.

Cal: That's what makes him an amazing songwriter. We only found out about Kill's songs about a year or so ago.

Carla: I've compiled a list of things my readers want to know about The Blind Rebels. So I'm going to give you the question and if you'd all just give me your answers for each.

Carla: Favorite Cereal?

Mav: I don't eat cereal. I'm more of an eggs or avocado toast kind of guy.

Cal: Special K or oatmeal.

Sammy: Cap'n Crunch

Killian: Whatever Harmony's eating. This week I think it's Cinnamon Toast Crunch.

Carla: Favorite Drink?

Mav: If we're talking alcohol, whiskey neat.

Cal: Beer...or water.

Sammy: Gatorade. I'll have a beer sometimes, but I don't drink much.

Killian: I don't drink much either...I'll have a beer to be sociable.

Carla: What do you drink in the morning?

Mav: Coffee. The darker the roast the better.

Cal: Coffee. Any ol' kind.

Sammy: Usually Gatorade. Sometimes I'll sneak one of Melody's Monster Ultras.

Killian: If I'm home, I'll have coffee with Vi. Other than that, just water.

Carla: Hot dogs or cheeseburgers?

Mav: Steak or cheeseburger, but I'd rather have steak.

Cal: Cheeseburger.

Sammy: Both!

Killian: Um, probably cheeseburger.

Carla: Last food related one, what's your favorite type of food?

Mav, Cal, and Killian all answer at once: Mexican.

Sammy: All of it.

Carla: Can you swim?

Mav: I can answer this for all of us. Yes, we all swim. We all surf. All our wives and children can swim. There are a few of the Rebel kids that don't *love* to swim, especially my son Brio but everyone *can* swim because we all have pools, and we all do water-based activities together.

Carla: A few of our readers wanted to know if any of you can do 100 push-ups?

Cal: I can. I'm pretty sure Sammy could if we dared him. I don't think the other guys care to find out.

Carla: What's your favorite tattoo?

Mav: Probably still my first- the microphone on my bicep that says Blind Rebels under it. But then again- I have the

241

fewest of the band.

Cal: I'm working with my tattoo artist now on one that will include all three of my kids. That's my favorite and I don't even have it yet.

Sammy: I have a wave on my back shoulder that's got Melody's name written in the foam.

Killian: I have three favorites. The paintbrushes over my heart that represent my wife, the mermaid on my thigh that Harmony designed, and the Fender bass on my back that represents this little guy here.

Carla: Okay, one last one. Do you believe in ghosts?

Mav: No.

Cal: Not really, no.

Sammy: Yes.

Killian: I'm not sure.

Mav: Those were some awesome questions your readers came up with. Please thank them for coming up with them!

Carla: Will do! I love including them in interviews as much as possible.

So there you've heard about the upcoming release right from the Blind Rebels themselves. Keep rockin' and reading the latest music news here on Rock & Metal Round Up.

The Playlist

I've made playlists for each of the Blind Rebel books. The playlist for *Blurring the Lines (as well as all of the Blind Rebel books)* can be found on my Spotify.

This is a small sampling of the songs found on the Spotify playlist for *Blurring the Lines*:

1. Zombie- Bad Wolves
2. Gone Away- Five Finger Death Punch
3. Angel- Theory of a Deadman
4. Burn it to the Ground - Nickelback
5. Help- Papa Roach
6. Fake It- Seether
7. In The End- Black Veil Brides
8. Break- Three Days Grace
9. Addicted- Saving Abel
10. Headstrong- Trapt

You can find me and all of my playlists on Spotify: Amy Kaybach

Acknowledgments

A special thank you and huge virtual hug of appreciation to those who went through several different iterations of this manuscript because there were so many different versions of this story to get to just the right one.

The first couple of attempts at this novella just didn't hit right so a big thank you for your patience and help go to **Best Friend Misty™**, **Shayna Astor** and **Sherry Bessette** for reading, and rereading and then rereading the novella again.

Also thank you to:

- **My ARC readers & Bookstagrammers who help get the word out:** Your support means the world to me! I love seeing all of your content on social media. It makes my day better when I'm tagged or run across your content promoting my books. I'm especially looking at you **Kristen, Lexi and Amanda!**
- **Jamie:** I hope you're ready for more- I have so many ideas. And thank you always for planting the little seed that maybe I should consider publishing! But mostly thank you for being my friend!
- **Tricia:** For your undying and enthusiastic support and reads in the rough form.
- **Kimberly Sable:** This cover is so beautiful and so fitting for the prequel to the series. Thank you for working with me to get it just right!

- **Hayleigh of Editing Fox:** Thank you always believing in me and my characters and working with me to make them even better.
- **Mackenzie of Nice Girl, Naughty Edits:** Still working on learning correct comma use.
- **Charli of Charli's Book Box:** Thank you for your continued help with my web page and your awesome support for my books and my Rebel boys!

About the Author

Amy Kaybach is a romance author from the central coast of California.

Begging her parents when she was three to teach her to "write words," Amy's loved writing since she can remember. She also learned to read early and quickly fell in love with the worlds in her books. Once, a precocious ten-year-old Amy frustrated her mom so much that she took away Amy's books instead of television because Amy didn't really care about what was on TV anyway.

When she is not writing or dreaming about sexy rockstars, Amy is working in information technology communications or dreaming of her next grand adventure.

Amy is owned by two obnoxious but well-loved albeit spoiled beagles, Abbie and Gracie.

Amy adores interacting with readers (yes that means you)! Contact her on her social media:

Also by Amy Kaybach

The Blind Rebels rock star romance series:

Bridging the Silence (Blind Rebels book 1)

Blending Chords (Blind Rebels book 2)

Reviving the Rhythm (Blind Rebels book 3)

Finding Harmony (Blind Rebels book 4)